7 BILLION LIVES ARE IN DANGER.
13 STRANGERS WITH TERRIFYING NIGHTMARES.
1 ENEMY WILL STOP AT NOTHING TO DESTROY US ALL.

MY NAME IS SAM.
I AM ONE OF THE LAST THIRTEEN.
OUR BATTLE CONTINUES.

Sch $12.00.

This one's for Jesse—an excellent Pete and occasional traitor—JP.

Scholastic Australia
345 Pacific Highway Lindfield NSW 2070
An imprint of Scholastic Australia Pty Limited
PO Box 579 Gosford NSW 2250
ABN 11 000 614 577
www.scholastic.com.au

Part of the Scholastic Group
Sydney • Auckland • New York • Toronto • London • Mexico City
• New Delhi • Hong Kong • Buenos Aires • Puerto Rico

Published by Scholastic Australia in 2014.
Text copyright © James Phelan, 2014.
Illustrations & design copyright © Scholastic Australia, 2014.
Illustrations by Chad Mitchell. Design by Nicole Stofberg.

Cover photography: Blueprint © istockphoto.com/Adam Korzekwa; Parkour Tic-Tac © istockphoto.com/Willie B. Thomas;
Climbing wall © istockphoto.com/microgen; Leonardo da Vinci (Sepia) © istockphoto.com/pictore; Gears © istockphoto.com/
Oxford-; Mechanical blueprint © istockphoto.com/teekid; Circuit board © istockphoto.com/Bjorn Meyer; Map © istockphoto.
com/alengo; Grunge drawing © istockphoto.com/aleksandar velasevic; World map © istockphoto.com/Maksim Pasko; Internet
© istockphoto.com/Andrey Prokhorov; Inside clock © istockphoto.com/LdF; Space galaxy © istockphoto.com/Sergii Tsololo;
Sunset © istockphoto.com/Joakim Leroy; Blue flare © istockphoto.com/YouraPechkin; Global communication © istockphoto.
com/chadive samanthakamani; Earth satellites © istockphoto.com/Alexey Popov; Girl portrait © istockphoto.com/peter zelei;
Student & board © istockphoto.com/zhang bo; Young man serious © istockphoto.com/Jacob Wackerhausen; Portrait man ©
istockphoto.com/Alina Solovyova-Vincent; Sad expression © istockphoto.com/Shelly Perry; Content man © istockphoto.com/
drbimages; Pensive man © istockphoto.com/Chuck Schmidt; Black and pink © istockphoto.com/blackwaterimages; Punk Girl ©
istockphoto.com/Kuzma; Woman escaping © Jose antonio Sanchez reyes/Photos.com; Young running man © Tatiana Belova/
Photos.com; Gears clock © Jupiterimages/Photos.com; Woman portrait © Sanjay Deva/Photos.com; Explosions © Leigh
Prather | Dreamstime.com; Landscape blueprints © Firebrandphotography | Dreamstime.com; Jump over wall © Ammentorp
| Dreamstime.com; Mountains, CAN © Akadiusz Iwanicki | Dreamstime.com; Sphinx Bucegi © Adrian Nicolae | Dreamstime.
com; Big mountains © Hoptrop | Dreamstime.com; Sunset mountains © Pklimenko | Dreamstime.com; Mountains lake ©
Janmika | Dreamstime.com; Blue night sky © Mack2happy | Dreamstime.com; Old writing © Empire331 | Dreamstime.com;
Young man © Shuen Ho Wang | Dreamstime.com; Abstract cells © Sur | Dreamstime.com; Helicopter © Evren Kalinbacak |
Dreamstime.com; Aeroplane © Rgbe | Dreamstime.com; Phrenology illustration © Mcarrel | Dreamstime.com; Abstract interior
© Sur | Dreamstime.com; Papyrus © Cebreros | Dreamstime.com; Blue shades © Mohamed Osama | Dreamstime.com; Blue
background © Matusciac | Dreamstime.com; Sphinx and Pyramid © Dan Breckwoldt | Dreamstime.com; Blue background2
© Cammeraydave | Dreamstime.com; Abstract shapes © Lisa Mckown | Dreamstime.com; Yellow Field © Simon Greig |
Dreamstime.com; Blue background3 © Sergey Skrebnev | Dreamstime.com; Blue eye © Richard Thomas | Dreamstime.com;
Abstract landscape © Crazy80frog | Dreamstime.com; Rameses II © Jose I. Soto | Dreamstime.com; Helicopter © Sculpies |
Dreamstime.com; Vitruvian man © Cornelius20 | Dreamstime.com; Scarab beetle © Charon | Dreamstime.com; Eye of Horus
© Charon | Dreamstime.com; Handsome male portrait © DigitalHand Studio/Shutterstock.com; Teen girl © CREATISTA/
Shutterstock.com; Floating gate © Callousius | Dreamstime.com; Tokyo © Marcio Silva | Dreamstime.com; Samurai © Ivan
Demyanov | Dreamstime.com; Sports car © Stuart Key | Dreamstime.com; Warrior training in sunset © Zurijeta | Dreamstime.
com; Sunset and cherry blossoms © Voyager624 | Dreamstime.com; Japanese writing on rock © Sam Dcruz/Shutterstock.com;
Sea/wave breaker © Sam Dcruz/Shutterstock.com; Coral reef © Yonaguni Island, Okinawa, Japan © Sam Dcruz/Shutterstock.
com; Sea - Yonaguni Island, Okinawa, Japan © Sam Dcruz/Shutterstock.com; Hashima Island (Gunkan Island), Nagasaki
Prefecture, Kyushu, Japan © NAOFUMI KUROKI/a.collectionRF; View of Battlehsip Island © TRUE2DEATH; Battleship Island ©
2011 tomosang; Atomic dome © istockphoto.com/holgs; Home of ash © istockphoto.com/Biscut; Commuting © istockphoto.
com/sack; In the subway station © istockphoto.com/kokouu; Tokyo transit system line © istockphoto.com/holgs; Train station 2
© istockphoto.com/sack; Hectic city life in Tokyo © istockphoto.com/wingmar; Tokyo towers in moonlight © istockphoto.com/
EscoLux; Surreal view of Yokohama and Mt. Fuji © istockphoto.com/shirophoto; Tokyo Shibuya crossing © istockphoto.com/
Nikada; Tokyo tower © istockphoto.com/TommL; Surreal view of rainbow bridge and Mt. Fuji © istockphoto.com/shirophoto.
Internal photography: p06, Tablet © Jbk_photography | Dreamstime.com; p09, Hanging street banner © Wuka | Dreamstime.
com; p79, Construction ahead sign © stevezmina1/istockphoto.com; p125, Old and worn painted sign © Simon Greig |
Dreamstime.com, Graffiti spray paint font, parts 1, 2 and 3 © Foreks | Dreamstime.com; p150, TV news reporter © Rui Matos |
Dreamstime.com, Breaking news © Rasà Messina Francesca | Dreamstime.com.

A Cataloguing-in-Publication entry is available from the National Library of Australia.

Typeset in Esperanto and Interstate.

Printed by McPherson's Printing Group, Maryborough, Victoria.
Scholastic Australia's policy, in association with McPherson's Printing Group, is to use papers that are renewable and made
efficiently from wood grown in sustainable forests, so as to minimise its environmental footprint.

10 9 8 7 6 5 4 3 2   14 15 16 17 18 / 1

THE LAST THIRTEEN

BOOK NINE

JAMES PHELAN

A Scholastic Australia Book

PREVIOUSLY

As the bomb threatens to explode, Solaris unexpectedly gives Sam back the Gears Mac stole from him. Sam manages to break free and flee the Denver site in an escape pod before blacking out.

Sam has strange dreams he does not understand, until he is woken by the next Dreamer, Arianna. She rescues him from a Hypnos centre in Moscow, revealing she is a Nyx, and has had her dreams taken from her. Fleeing to the Kremlin to seek help, they are double-crossed and have to run from the Hypnos and Hans, who has stolen Arianna's Gear.

Alex and Shiva try to realise Tesla's dream of tapping into the Dreamscape by reactivating his Coils in a long-abandoned Dreamer warehouse in New York. Siphoning off power from City Hall, they succeed in bringing the Coils online, only to have them explode spectacularly, knocking them both unconscious.

Eva learns about a Dreamer contest called the Four Corners Competition at the Academy's London campus. Cody arrives and she interrogates him about what happened in Denver. After Eva dreams of a thirteen-symbol zodiac, the Professor urges her to go with Dr Dark to investigate its significance. However, when Dr Kader comes aboard their plane to New York, Eva pulls a gun on him, knowing he has betrayed Sam.

❀

Sam and Arianna travel to Siberia by train, where Arianna and the Nyx are planning an assault on the Hypnos base there. But before they can attack, Hans kidnaps them both, drugging Sam to force him to dream.

❀

Alex comes to in a New York hospital, to be questioned by the same two cops he met there before. He does some fast-talking to get himself and Shiva released, returning to Shiva's apartment to regroup. On their way back to the warehouse, they're confronted by Stella and Matrix.

❀

Sam fights to control his dreams and to give nothing away to Hans. Awakening, he's trapped in a cell with a fire breaking out all around him. There is no way to escape as the flames close in . . .

SAM

Outside the room the fire raged.

Sweat ran down Sam's face. He started to hyper-ventilate.

Stay calm.

Smoke seeped under the door, filling the room with a black haze. Sam returned to the bed and tore off the bottom of the sheet. He ran to the small basin in the corner of the room and soaked the cloth, wrapping it around his mouth and nose and tying it behind his head. He kept low, frantically searching the bare room for anything that might help him escape.

The bed?

He checked the bedframe and the sturdy legs underneath.

Metal. I could try to break it apart, use part of the metal frame as a crowbar to prise open the door . . .

BANG!

Sam looked at the door. Through the small window he could see a black mask staring at him through the billowing smoke.

No!

Sam paused.

That's not Solaris.

He rushed to the mesh grill to look closer. The mask was a gas mask, with a large clear visor covering the eyes. Even with his mind cloudy, he knew those eyes.

Arianna!

She pointed at him and then made a shooing motion.

Get away from the door—right!

Sam quickly jumped back to the other side of the room.

BOOM! BOOM! BOOM!

Tiny explosives detonated in quick succession and the door was blown clear off its hinges, flying across the room and hitting the wall opposite, mere centimetres from where Sam stood.

'Wow!' Sam said, impressed.

Arianna rushed into the room and, without speaking, pulled a dart pistol from a holster strapped to her thigh and shot him in the arm. He looked down at the dart.

What . . ? Why would she . . ?

He felt a rush of adrenalin, and was immediately more awake than he could ever remember feeling.

'Put this on!' Arianna yelled at Sam, taking another gas mask from her pack. 'And stay close behind me!'

Sam put on the mask and shadowed Arianna as they made their way down the hallway through clearing smoke.

Is the fire out now?

In a large office two doors away, Sam could see Hans lying on the ground, unconscious. Just then, a Hypnos soldier staggered towards them from within the wall of dense smoke ahead, gun in hand.

Arianna reacted fast.

Swiftly, looking just like the gymnast he knew her to be, Sam watched as she cartwheeled in a heartbeat, kicking the guy with her flying foot. He fell to the ground unconscious. Two more soldiers followed close behind, and she moved just as quickly. This time Sam was with her. Together they jumped—a twist, a kick, dart guns firing and it was all over.

Arianna's a gymnastic ninja! Glad she's on my side.

'We have to go!' Arianna said, her eyes anxious through her visor.

'Wait!'

Sam bent down to Hans and took the small case he still clutched in one hand. Flipping the lid, Sam could see the Gears, retrieved from Brazil and Cuba, and also Cody's from America. And there was one more—

'That's mine. Stolen from me, taken from my stolen dream. Now we take it *back*,' Arianna said defiantly.

Sam nodded and smiled. He picked up the case, closing it carefully and tucking it under his arm. 'Time to go.'

We're really back in the race now.

'How much can you remember about what happened?' Arianna asked him as the car bumped along the dirt road. Sam thought about the question and had a strange sense of deja vu.

'You gave me a shot in my arm, adrenalin, I think,' he said, still watching through his side window. 'There was all that fire and smoke as we ran out from the building, just before a big explosion.'

He sat next to Arianna in the back of a four-wheel drive, Boris at the wheel. They'd been driving for an hour, heading south-east to the closest border.

'It wasn't just adrenalin,' Arianna said. 'It was also the antidote to the memory-blocker they gave you.'

'Well, whatever it was,' Sam said, 'I'm *really* awake now. One thing I'm sure I remember—you were trapped with me, right? Tied up like I was . . . what happened after I started dreaming? How did you . . ?'

Arianna grinned. 'There was one thing Hans was not expecting—we had a member of the Nyx working inside the compound. A secret weapon, you would say?'

Sam nodded. 'Yes, I would say! But you and Boris never mentioned having someone on the inside.'

'I'm sorry, we had to trust no-one to keep Oleg safe while he pretended to be with the Hypnos. Only a handful of us even knew he was there,' Arianna said. 'When we were captured, he was there to set me free and I came looking for you. I hoped to find you before you dreamed too long or forgot too much.'

'And I'm *very* grateful, believe me. But my memories *are* still foggy.'

'It will take up to twenty-four hours for the Hypnos' drug to get out of your system,' Arianna explained. 'It'll help if you keep reading those notes,' she added.

Sam nodded and read over the notes on the tablet screen—all kinds of collected data on the last 13.

'Well,' Arianna said to Boris, 'that rescue went better than I thought.'

Boris nodded in agreement but his eyes did not leave the road.

Sam looked to Arianna and then to Boris. 'What did you think would happen? It seemed pretty full-on to me.'

'Well, not all the Hypnos sites across the country fell so easily,' Arianna said. 'There were heavy casualties on both sides. But, as far as we know, all the sites have been destroyed by the Nyx.'

'That sounds amazing.'

Nyx are the good guys, Hypnos are the bad guys, Sam

remembered. He looked down at the case holding the Gears.

Like Hans. And . . . Stella, and Solaris. They all want these, we can't let them get the Gears back. Hang on, who's we . . ?

'My friends! I need to return to the Academy,' Sam said urgently.

'We know,' Boris replied in halting English. 'We drive for airport.'

Sam relaxed a little and nodded. He started to smile as a face came to mind—Eva. And there were others, part of the last 13, he was sure. He went back to reading, slotting together more missing memories, returning to him slowly piece by piece. He pulled up a new file on screen.

THE LAST 13 UPDATE

The Professor of the Academy informed the Council that Sam continues to be the pivotal figure of the last 13; the only one who can dream of these 13 special Dreamers from anywhere around the world. To date, Sam has been instrumental in finding Dreamers in France, Germany, Italy, South America, Cuba and the United States, and in uncovering Gears in each of these locations. The Dreamers found so far

Sam couldn't clearly remember being in any of those places, but as the names and the faces of the other Dreamers followed, he started to recognise them. Other files, from reports of his time in Germany, showed a very different face to the one he saw in the reflection of the tablet computer's screen.

Was I in disguise in Germany?

Sam touched the back of his head—it was shaved, but there was no scar.

It was only a dream.

'Thank you,' Sam said to Arianna. 'For everything.'

'You're welcome,' Arianna replied. 'You should get some rest.'

Sam nodded. 'Will I dream yet?' he said.

Arianna paused. 'Maybe . . . probably.'

'Has—has destroying the Hypnos' facilities changed *everything*?' he asked her. 'Will *you* dream again? And remember your dreams?'

Arianna smiled and Sam saw tears well in her eyes when she said, 'Yes.'

SAM'S NIGHTMARE

It is so bright that I feel like I'm looking into the sun. Voices shout out over the top of one other—some in English, others in a very different language. It's Japanese, I think.

'Issey—over here!'

'Good luck, Issey!'

'Smile!'

I shield my eyes with a raised hand—the bright lights all around me are camera flashes.

Dozens of them, like the paparazzi mobs I've seen on TV. They're all pointing in my direction, the incessant flashes so close together it's like a constant blinding blaze. Issey is behind me. I turn to look at him. Wow. He's probably one of the coolest guys I've ever seen.

Actually, no. Issey is by far and away the coolest guy I've ever seen.

Looking around me at the neon-blazing signs towering in every direction, I take an educated guess—we are in the middle of Tokyo. Issey is walking down the red carpet rolled out in front of us, his black spiky hair perfectly styled. He wears skinny black jeans and a leather jacket that a racing driver would be proud of. It's covered in logos and brand names, seemingly every major company in the world sponsoring him so they get to be part of his publicity machine. His shoes are bright blue hi-tops and he's wearing huge black sunglasses—he is a rock star.

But he isn't a musician or singer, and he's not a famous actor either—think, Sam . . . what happened before in the dream?

The memory comes back to me—Issey is a professional gamer.

That's it. I knew I'd seen his face somewhere before. All those guest spots in music videos.

Someone yells out, 'Issey, I love you!'

I feel underdressed, self-conscious and geeky around him. We're on the red carpet together with his full entourage, but I don't belong in this world. I hang back as I look up at the hulking structure before us. As we head into the giant stadium through the wide open doors, Issey stops beneath a sign for final photographs and questions.

'Issey, do you think you can win the tournament again?' a reporter yells out.

'Well . . .' Issey smiles.

'It's been three years in a row now,' another reporter interrupts. 'Has your luck run out?'

'Ha! Luck? I'm going to smash them all—again!' Issey replies, raising his fist into the air, and the crowd goes wild with cheers. He strides away, confidence oozing from every pore.

I jog to catch up to him and his group inside, trying to clear the ringing out of my ears. I see Lora shadowing me through the crowd, keeping a lookout.

The games arena is in a sports centre. A huge crowd, maybe ten thousand people are seated around, all eyes on Issey as he makes his entrance. Giant screens show close-ups of the court below, ready to show all the action.

In the centre of the court is a raised stage with two banks of computer equipment facing each other. A red team and a blue team. Video cameras and crews are everywhere.

Issey is leading the red team.

Looking up at the scoreboard, I see a girl named Psy is commanding the five-member blue team.

'Ah, Issey,' I say, 'what are you guys playing?'

'Playing? No, we don't play. This may be gaming, but it's not playing—this is real, this is high stakes.'

He points to a glass cube hanging above the winner's podium.

'Million bucks for the winner,' he says.

'Wow.'

'And *that*.'

He points to an orange tricked-out super sports car.

'Double wow,' I say. 'Think you can really win this tournament?'

'The Koreans,' Issey says to me, motioning with his head across the floor, 'are our biggest threat. I'm not surprised they made it to the finals.'

I look at the Korean team members in matching uniforms, sitting at their consoles. They don't look like a threat—they look twelve, maybe thirteen years old at most. They all have crazy hairdos and sunglasses—they look more like a pop band.

The announcer says something in Japanese, then repeats it in English, 'Ladies and gentlemen, boys and girls, geeks and gamers, welcome to the annual Pan Pacific Gaming Smackdown!'

The crowd goes crazy.

'All this is for you?' I ask. 'Really, for gamers?'

'Yeah, it's always like this.'

'Unreal, I guess I didn't get how big this was.'

Issey looks at me, and then he turns to the audience members nearest to us and raises his fists into the air. The crowd's cheering reaches fever-pitch, as if Issey really is the world's greatest rock star.

Must be his signature move.

Just then, as I'm looking at Issey, the lights go out. All the power in the arena shuts down—screens, advertising signs, everything.

BANG! BANG! BANG!

Each section of the stadium, one by one, goes dark.

After a moment of silence, an emergency generator kicks in, illuminating the exits with dim strip lighting.

'Maybe all this tech gear overloaded the power—' I say, stopping abruptly, as screams begin to echo in the half-light. At first it comes from a few people at the back of the crowd. Then dozens, then hundreds of people. Terrified screams swirl around the stadium from all directions.

Commotion and mayhem erupts as thousands of people begin rushing for the exits. Others are running in the opposite direction. They don't look like they're trying to get out, they look like they're trying to get away—*from* something.

I hear a howl.

A strange sound that doesn't seem real. It's no animal that I recognise. It sounds like a monster or dinosaur from a bad movie . . .

'Issey, we have to get out of here!' I say.

Issey doesn't answer. He's frozen, transfixed by the scene around us. Many of the panicking crowd have switched on the lights in their phones, and the small pricks of light flash and dart around the gloom.

Through the shifting light I realise the true horror of what is happening.

'Lora!' I scream, searching through the tidal wave of people pushing past. Huge, unfamiliar shapes are moving randomly through the dark.

What are they?

Unbelievably, monstrous beasts are pouncing on people, dragging them down.

I want to close my eyes and block it out, but there's a new fear—the flash and heat of fire washing over me.

'Sam . . .' that familiar voice says. 'Do you like my . . . *pets?*' His booming laugh stabs into every part of my brain as everything is—

Torn apart.

SAM

'**A**rgh!' Sam jumped awake suddenly. His body ached as he tried to move out of the awkward position he'd been contorted in on the back seat of the car. The sun streaming through the window was hot on his face and he was sweating through his clothes. The seatbelt had dug into his shoulder, leaving a red welt. The car was stationary, parked someplace he didn't recognise.

I did dream again, he thought, relieved.

It was just a bad dream, shake it off. Monsters don't exist . . . it's people I have to worry about.

And yet it had been a good dream, too.

Japan. Issey.

As his senses slowly emerged from sleepiness, more memories came flooding back.

The last 13. I am one of them. This race will finish at the Dream Gate . . .

'Sam? Are you OK?' a voice said.

'Yeah.' Sam sat up on the back seat of the battered old car. Arianna was twisted around in the passenger seat, smiling at him.

'You were dreaming, a nightmare I think,' Arianna said kindly. 'But I didn't want to wake you . . .'

'Ah, yeah. Sorry,' Sam said, sitting up straighter and rubbing the sleep from his eyes.

'Well, it is a good time to wake,' Arianna said, pointing out the windscreen. 'We're here.'

Sam noticed the driver's seat was empty—Boris was gone. But then Sam saw him outside crossing the road.

'We're at the airport,' Arianna said. 'You slept most of the way. Boris has gone to check that all is clear.'

Sam nodded, watching the big Russian weaving casually through the busy commuter traffic. 'Was I, ah, talking, you know, in my sleep?' he said. He wondered how much he may have said out loud, and if any of it had been coherent.

'You spoke a little, at the end,' Arianna said in her heavy Russian accent. 'Mostly you keep saying, "No, no, no".'

'Kept.'

'Sorry?'

'Nothing, *I'm* sorry.' Sam wound his window down and let the cool morning air blow in. It stung at his face, the temperature easily in the negatives, with plenty of snow outside, and it woke him better than a dozen coffees. 'I was having a nightmare,' he admitted to Arianna. 'I was having this dream, and it became really weird.'

'How?'

'Well, Solaris was there, so that was the same. But this one had some kind of—monsters, I guess—in it.'

'Monsters?'

'Yeah. Like huge beasts, but nothing that I could recognise. They belonged to *him*.'

'I had a nightmare too,' Arianna said quietly.

'Sucks, doesn't it?' Sam said, and then the realisation hit him. 'Wait—you *dreamed* as well?'

'Yep,' Arianna said, smiling widely. 'For the first time in so long. And I can remember it!'

'That's *amazing!*' Sam said.

'It *was* so amazing!' Arianna said, sounding excited to have gotten back her ability to dream. 'It feels so unusual, but wonderful all at once. The nightmare, although, not so much . . .'

Sam nodded. 'The Academy told me the Dreamscape is full of nightmares right now, more than ever. It's because of the race.'

The car door opened and Boris got in, handing them both paper bags. The bag felt warm and when Sam opened it and looked inside, he was very happy to see a bread roll stuffed with coleslaw and pastrami. He realised then just how hungry he was.

'All is clear out there,' Boris said.

Sam nodded his thanks and said through a mouthful to Arianna, 'So that means that when you shut down the Hypnos' lab in Siberia . . .'

'That it deactivated the chip they implanted in Dreamers like me,' Arianna said. 'Just imagine all the people across the country who are now dreaming, who had no idea that we were moving against the Hypnos.'

Boris chuckled and said something in Russian. Sam looked to Arianna.

'He said they will know now,' Arianna translated. 'They will be thankful for what we've done. Here, use this,' she handed Sam a new earpiece translator, identical to the first.

'What happened in there?' Sam asked, as he inserted it into his ear. 'I mean, afterwards, to the guards at the lab?'

'The police found them this morning,' Boris said, smiling. 'I tipped them off.'

'What about Hans?' Sam asked. 'Think he will go to jail?'

'No, not yet,' Arianna said as Boris took off into the traffic to take them round to the airport's departure area. 'We left him at the facility, but still he managed to escape.'

'Big surprise . . .' Sam said, staring out his window.

Hans is probably halfway around the world by now, already planning his next move against us.

'We will continue to hunt this Hans,' Boris said, 'along with anyone still working for him or the Hypnos. After what we did at the Tunguska facility, he might find those who were willing to help him are now not so easily bought.'

'But at least we have these,' Sam said, looking at the Gears in the case. 'Which means there're only five left to find. Five, and then we have to find a way to get the other Gears from Solaris. Unless we have all thirteen Gears there's no way to assemble the Bakhu machine.' Sam paused, feeling overwhelmed as he thought about the seemingly insurmountable challenge ahead.

One step at a time, Sam. Just think about right now . . . the very next step.

'So now we're going back to the Academy? I mean, you're coming with me, right?' Sam asked Arianna.

'Your plane leaves very soon,' Boris answered, idling the car's engine at the drop-off point at the Departures terminal. A plane roared overhead. 'In a few hours you will be back in London.'

'Arianna?' Sam said.

'I should stay here, help Boris and the Nyx. But yes, Sam, I will join you. I understand my path now is to help win the race.'

They all got out, Sam tightly holding onto the box containing the Gears. He went to shake Boris' hand but the big bear of a man pulled him in for a rib-crushing hug instead.

'See you again, someday—soon, Sam.'

'Thanks, Boris, for everything.'

Arianna said goodbye to her friend, getting a bear hug of her own, and then she and Sam walked out of the icy wind and into the warm terminal.

Once inside, Sam saw two people running towards him. *Lora and Eva?*

'Hey, guys. Hi!' Sam exclaimed, before he was almost knocked to the ground as Eva flung herself onto him.

'Where've you been? We've been worried to death!' Eva said, pulling back and punching him in the arm.

'Ow! Hey, it wasn't by choice, I assure you,' Sam said. 'But I'm glad to see you missed me,' he grinned. He quickly introduced them to Arianna, who greeted them with firm handshakes and a warm smile. 'But what are *you* doing here?' he continued.

'We were on the way back to the Academy too,' Eva said. 'Heard you had reappeared in Russia so we took a detour to meet you.'

'Been on a holiday?' Sam joked.

'I was on a mission of my own, actually,' Eva said, punching his shoulder again, 'with Dr Dark and your old friend Ahmed Kader.'

'*What?*' Sam stopped in his tracks. 'But, but he—'

'Come on, you two,' Lora interrupted. 'We can catch up on everything on the plane. We're going to miss our flight if we don't hustle.'

ALEX

'What if I run really fast?' Alex said. 'You really think this wristband will blow my hand off?' He looked at the metal wristband, its little red blinking lights a constant reminder that he was a captive.

'You might make it down the hall and to the elevator,' Shiva replied. 'But most definitely, yes, it has enough explosive force to take your hand off and make a real mess of the rest of you.'

Alex let out a sigh. 'And if we try to get it off . . .'

'It has an anti-tamper mechanism that will start the timer, and if it's not reset in five minutes, *boom!*'

'Great, just great.'

'Could be worse.'

'How'd you figure?'

'At least we're in a nice apartment,' Shiva said.

'Yeah, I guess . . .' Alex looked around. They were sitting on beanbags in front of a TV screen that nearly took up the whole lounge room wall. But there was no internet or phone, and the windows were thick, locked tight and blacked out—so there was no use using the lights to signal for help to neighbouring buildings. They were in a luxury prison, sixty floors up. Alex could just make out the skyline of midtown Manhattan if he squinted through a tiny gap in the window. Cut off from the outside world with nothing but each other and just enough food to survive. No guards to watch over them, just the wristbands packed with explosives.

How can we be in the middle of the city with no neighbours? What is this building? Have we really been here a whole week? Man . . .

'You really don't think Phoebe or Jack will find us?'

'No, I think they would have found us by now if they were going to.'

'I know, I know,' Alex said. 'Sorry, man. I know we've been over this a hundred times. And speaking of things we've talked about before, what *do* you think Stella and Matrix are going to do with us?'

'My guess,' Shiva replied, 'is that they need you for something.'

'Me?'

'Maybe. It did look like you might be one of the last 13.'

'And then again, maybe not,' Alex sighed. 'Nothing's happened since the Professor and the Director told me that my dreaming patterns altered around the Gears. Nothing, zip.'

'Well, they won't take that chance.'

'Right,' Alex said. 'And what about you?'

Shiva shrugged.

'I mean, Stella wouldn't hurt you, right? With your skills, you're an asset to them,' Alex said. 'And Matrix wouldn't—'

'Yes, he *would*,' Shiva said.

Alex frowned, not knowing what to say.

'Don't worry about it, I'm not. You can't stop crazy people from doing stupid things. No doubt they've been over all that work that we did and have done some tinkering of their own.'

'They've had days to get it all right,' Alex sighed, exasperated.

'Exactly. So if Matrix can take over from where we finished, well . . . they'll have no use for me.'

'*If* they get it working,' Alex said.

Shiva nodded.

Alex swallowed hard. 'How much longer do you think it'll take them to get it online?'

'Soon, possibly in the next day or two,' Shiva replied straightaway, as though he'd calculated it long ago. 'The work we were doing was just testing the power supply. They'll have completed that and moved to the next stage.'

'Making them operational?'

Shiva nodded.

Alex said, 'And then they can tap into the Dreamscape, find Sam and the last 13, and this could all be over . . .'

Shiva nodded.

Alex stood. 'We gotta think up a new way out of this mess.'

'Seriously, the red wire?' Alex said.

They were looking inside his explosive wristband. The face of it had been painstakingly removed, one tiny screw at a time. Shiva had sharpened the end of the metal arm of his glasses, forming a screwdriver. Alex held an empty drinking glass overhead as an improvised magnifier so that Shiva could carefully re-route the anti-tamper wire with a longer piece that they'd removed from the TV console. Now they saw the small detonator and putty-like explosives that packed every bit of space inside the wristband. There were two wires, one red and one blue, which led from a small battery to the detonator.

Alex looked at the two wires. A simple choice lay before them—cut one or the other.

Cut the right wire, disable the device.

Cut the wrong one . . . boom.

A snip of a wire—device deactivated.

Or . . . the timer will start.

'What,' Shiva said, 'you think I should cut the blue wire?'

'I think that's what I've seen done before.'

'You've seen this done before?' Shiva said. 'And you're just telling me that *now*?'

'Well, yeah, kind of,' Alex said, keeping his arm completely steady under the bright lamplight. He didn't dare risk moving it while Shiva was working. 'In a movie,' he added quietly.

'A *movie?*'

'Yep.'

'Hmm. Which movie?'

'Can't remember. Does it matter?'

'Maybe. If it was a good movie, maybe I'd trust it. Did they succeed?'

'I think so. Or—or maybe not.'

'Cool, well, thanks for sharing, that was a big help.'

'No problem.' Alex swallowed hard. 'Hey, tell me again why we can't cut the wristband?'

'Well,' Shiva replied, 'for one thing, it's made of a titanium alloy, similar to what they use to make tank armour, so we'd need a serious diamond-cutting disc on an angle grinder and the bomb would go off before we got to a hardware store. Not to mention I might cut off your hand in the process.'

'Oh, right.'

'And, both wires seem to run *through* the wristband,' Shiva added, 'so if we cut or break the band, that would sever *both* wires and trigger the mechanism.'

'Oh, right,' Alex said. 'And thus trigger the anti-tamper . . . trigger.'

'Yeah, so let's not do that.'

'Agreed.' Alex blinked away at some sweat that was running into his eyes, focusing on the scene before him— his wrist, the bomb, and the nail clippers in Shiva's hands.

'OK. OK . . . let's do the wire,' Shiva said.

'The blue one, right?' Alex asked.

'Right.'

'I mean—wait, no, you said red before,' Alex said.

'And then you said blue,' Shiva corrected.

'Yeah—no, wait—did I?'

'You said something about a movie and that they cut either the red or the blue wire and it did or didn't go off,' Shiva said. 'But hey, if you think red, great, me too, totally, so let's cut the red wire.'

'You just said *blue!*'

SAM

Lora, Eva, Sam and Arianna arrived at the London campus of the Academy in time for dinner. Sam waited outside the dining hall, Lora, Eva and Arianna standing next to him. The hum of hundreds of students could be heard through the closed wooden doors.

'Can't I just take something to my room?' Sam said to Lora.

'You'll have to face them sooner or later,' Lora said. 'Better to get it over with. Go on in, I'll come and get you soon.'

'Yeah, I guess,' Sam said.

'What are you worried about?' Eva said, her hand on the door, slowly pushing it open. 'These past weeks you've been gone, no-one's barely noticed you were missing. Trust me, there's not going to be any crazy reception.'

Sam looked at her doubtfully.

They pushed the doors open.

The noisy chatter of a few hundred students at dinner died down, first quieting to whispers, and then stopping altogether. Silence. Sam could feel the stare of every set of eyes in the room that were locked on him.

What happened next reminded him of Issey's crazy fans from his nightmare. In unison, the Academy students erupted into cheers. They clapped and whooped and screamed, some stamping their feet while others used the cutlery to add to the raucous noise. He ducked his head in embarrassment and followed Eva to the table where the others of the last 13 sat. He shook hands and received hugs from his friends. As the noise in the hall eventually died down, Sam felt, for the first time since he could remember, like he was home.

Even as Sam was introducing Arianna to everyone, they could barely stop themselves from asking questions. Everyone at the table wanted to find out all about what happened to him in the US and Russia.

'We heard it was a full nuclear blast,' Xavier said, smirking. 'So, are you like a real radioactive superhero now?'

Sam rolled his eyes.

'Did a spider bite you?' Rapha asked, joking along. 'Can you climb walls?'

'Yeah, yeah,' Sam said, secretly grateful for the light-hearted moment. 'I did dream of wolves, though.'

'Wolf Boy,' Xavier said, grinning. 'Seriously, dude, how many lives do you have?'

'Thirteen,' Sam said without missing a beat.

'Wolf Boy is lame,' Gabriella laughed, joining in. 'We should have a competition to think up Sam's superhero name.'

'Whatever,' Sam said. 'And, thanks, you're really helping with this "go back to normal life afterward" idea that I had.'

'It's OK, Sam,' Zara said. 'You have been missing. We all miss you.'

'Some of us,' Xavier joked.

Maria hit him in the arm. 'Tell us what you've been doing,' she said. 'And don't leave out the good parts!'

He answered as many questions as he could, but asked many too—wanting to know what the others had been up to in his absence.

Sam had been uneasy about seeing Cody again and had tried not to pay him any attention during dinner. He noticed that everyone else at the table seemed to be happy enough to have him there. When Cody finally spoke up and added his side to Sam's story about the complex in Denver, describing for Sam's benefit how he and his parents ejected to safety, Sam just listened.

He seems genuinely sorry for leading me there. I guess he was really taken in by Mac. And his parents must have told him it was the right thing to do. Most of us believe our parents, don't we?

'And now what will your parents do?' Sam asked Cody.

'They, um, are working for the Enterprise again,' he answered quietly. 'They want to help in any way they can.

They know things that might be useful.' He paused before adding, 'Sam, I'm really—'

'Let's not talk about it now,' Sam cut him off. There was a long awkward silence at the table—no-one knew what to say next.

'And any word on Alex?' Sam asked finally, changing the subject.

Eva shook her head and said, 'He went missing, about the same time as you, along with the Enterprise tech guy, Shiva. They were in New York, working on old Dreamer stuff, apparently.'

'Oh . . .' Sam said.

'They'll be fine,' Xavier added. 'My father's sure of it. They'll find them.'

'Do they think Stella has anything to do with it?'

'We believe so,' Eva said, 'Stella *and* Matrix. The Director says it's clear now they wanted those Tesla Coils. They'll probably have set them up someplace hidden.'

'She won't hurt them,' Sam said, looking around the table at the faces of all his friends. He could see Gabriella was nodding, as she believed it too. 'They're both too valuable. She'll be keeping them to trade with us.'

'Trade?' Arianna asked.

'For something they need,' Sam said. 'The Gears, maybe.'

'Or one of us,' Xavier said.

The table fell silent.

Sam felt a presence behind him and turned around.

It was Lora.

'Sam, are you finished? Can you please accompany me to the Professor's office?' she asked.

'Sure.'

'Eva, you too.'

'Of course, yes,' Eva said, and they left the dining hall and its buzz of activity behind. Sam glanced back over his shoulder. He'd made some friends here, and he liked the atmosphere, the feeling of being around them. When he was here, with the other Dreamers, he felt he truly belonged. And that feeling was far removed from all that he had in the race—always running, hiding, trying to get to the next Dreamer and Gear before anyone else did. Here, he could just be himself.

Now that I know Issey is number nine, really it's just four more dreams. Four more dreams and we'll have found all 13 Dreamers and then this will be over . . . one way or another.

'**M**an,' Eva said once they were out in the corridor, 'that was *intense*. It's like you're a celebrity. Gabriella will get jealous!'

Lora laughed. 'They were worried about Sam,' she said. 'It's been so long since he was last here, many were preparing themselves for the worst news.'

'What,' Sam said, 'that I beat Solaris all on my own and everyone else missed out on the action?'

They laughed as they walked along the dimly lit corridors through the old school building.

'How about you guys?' Sam said, thinking about what Lora had said. 'Did you think I was toast? Or that I'd become some kind of radioactive superhero?'

'Never,' Eva said.

'Ah, that's my Dream Girl!' Sam said to Eva, getting her in a playful headlock. 'Always confident that I'll be there to fight another day.'

'No, I meant that I didn't think you'd ever be a superhero!' Eva replied. She easily wriggled out of the headlock and swiftly put Sam into one of her own.

'I see someone's been upping their combat skills since I've been gone,' Sam said, tapping out as she messed up his hair and let him go.

'I've been going to jujitsu classes,' Eva said. 'And studying up a bit—Combating Nightmares, How to Steer Your Unconscious Mind and all that. I had to do *something* while I was here or I would have gone crazy.'

'She's turned out to be quite the stellar student,' Lora said to Sam, opening the door to the Professor's office. 'You've got some catching up to do, Sam.'

'Yeah, I figured,' Sam said. 'Though it's hardly like I've been sitting on a couch in front of the TV all this time, either.'

'Yes, *we know*, you're running around, *saving* the world,' Eva said, and the three of them sat in the Professor's empty office. 'Hey, what's with your hair? It's like you've had a big chunk of it shaved off at the back.'

'Oh, this?' Sam said, touching where the Hypnos had prepped him for his dream chip implant. 'It's nothing, just a close encounter with a "Dream Ghoul".'

'A *what?*'

'I'm surprised you haven't read about them, what with all your studying,' Sam teased. 'Lora, you know all about them, right?'

'Oh, sure,' Lora said with a barely concealed smirk, 'Dream Ghouls, very nasty business. Especially when they scream.'

'They scream?' Eva said, shifting in her seat.

'The one that did this to me was the worst kind too,' Sam said. 'Lucky escape.'

Eva's face creased with concern.

Then Sam and Lora cracked up laughing.

'No, not really!' Sam admitted, and Eva tried to wrestle him into another headlock. Sam was ready this time and got free easily. 'I had you going for a minute, though, didn't I?'

Eva pulled a face at him. 'Stop clowning around! How *did* you get that shaved patch on the back of your head, then?'

Sam felt at the spiky crop of shaved hair and remembered back to when Hans and the Hypnos had drugged him. 'Some mad Russian scientist shaved it,' he said.

'Why would he do that?'

'Prepping me for an operation, I think. He was working for Hans. They were going to plant a chip in my brain, to steal my dreams.'

'Sam, I said stop clowning around!' Eva said, exasperated.

Sam grimaced. 'Actually, that time I wasn't. That's the truth.'

'Oh, right. Sorry,' Eva said. 'Well, you need a haircut. It looks weird like that.'

Sam laughed. 'I'll put it on my list.' Sam leaned over the arm of his chair and asked, 'So, tell me, what have you been doing apart from all those classes?'

'Well, I wasn't here the whole time. Lora and I nearly caught up with you in Colorado, but we were turned back from the airport as it was being evacuated.'

Sam was quiet for a moment. 'You were there?'

'Yes,' Lora said. 'Scary stuff.'

'You got out in an escape pod—do you think Solaris might have too?' Eva said.

'Maybe,' Sam said. 'Who knows?'

The door swung open.

'I'm here,' the Professor said, entering his office in a hurry. 'Sorry for the delay, had to put out a few fires.'

'Fires?' Sam said, shifting in his seat.

'Yes, metaphorically speaking, our world of dreams has gone, as you might say, nuts,' the Professor replied.

'I do believe that "nuts" is the technical term that we use,' Sam said sagely.

The Professor chuckled. 'Anyway, there are problems of nightmarish proportions breaking out all over the world. But it *is* good to see you, Sam, safe and well—apart from the haircut.'

'Yeah, I'm working on that.'

'As you can see, it's a chaotic time,' the Professor said, hanging his jacket and hat and sitting behind his desk. He seemed older to Sam, even though it was only a matter of weeks since he'd seen him last. Papers covered the Professor's desk, stacked high and haphazardly, a state of chaos that reminded Sam of his own desk back home, overflowing with schoolwork.

The Professor switched on a TV screen on the wall, leaving the volume turned down. A news channel was flicking between scenes of destruction in China, Spain and Greece. 'I'm sure you're already aware, Sam, that the world is falling to pieces with violence erupting everywhere, all sorts of extreme and unpredictable weather . . .'

'And it's because of the Dreamscape?' Sam said, watching the images on the screens. 'All this chaos?'

'Yes, I'm afraid so,' the Professor replied. 'The more that the population of the world suffers subconsciously in the realm of dreams, the more we will see unrest in waking life. Nowhere in the world is immune. There are reports of riots in East Asia and Europe, marches here in London that turned violent, wars breaking out across Africa, civil unrest throughout Argentina and Chile, chaos in Los Angeles . . .'

'The world's gone psycho . . .' Sam said, transfixed by the images on the screen. 'How can we fix it? *Can* we fix it?'

'Only by getting to the Dream Gate as quickly as we can,' the Professor said. 'Unlocking the power beyond is the only way to restore balance.'

'OK, well, we're back in the race,' Sam said, shifting forward in his seat, 'With Arianna's help, we've gotten back the Gears from Hans.'

'And Lora tells me that you have had your next dream,' the Professor said.

'Yes, the next Dreamer is called Issey. He's in Japan.'

'We've got all Issey's details,' Lora explained to the Professor, passing over a tablet computer. 'I had Jedi compile it when we were on the flight here.'

'Excellent,' the Professor said, scrolling through the information.

'We have a team of local Guardians secretly watching over him now,' Lora said. 'And Sam and I will leave for Tokyo tomorrow.'

The Professor nodded. 'Good. In the meantime, let us catch up on everything and prepare for what is next. I want no more surprises, and no more situations like Denver.'

'I couldn't agree more,' Sam said.

EVA

That night Eva could not sleep. Gabriella was now bunking with Zara since Gabriella could speak French and the two had bonded.

Fine with me.

Arianna was Eva's new roommate and she was talking in her sleep.

Clearly having a fun dream though, not a nightmare.

As if to confirm that thought, Arianna laughed on cue, then snorted, breathed heavily, rolled onto her side and finally fell quiet.

Maybe now I can get some sleep.

Eva closed her eyes, willing herself to sleep. Five minutes passed. Then ten, fifteen. Try as she might, her mind was too busy, racing with thoughts about Alex, about the Dream Coils, about the fruitless trip she'd taken last week with Dr Dark in search of the mysterious zodiac she had dreamed of.

My dream showed us that weird thirteen-symbol zodiac, but we couldn't find out anything more about it . . . maybe we were looking in the wrong place . . .

At least the trip had cleared up the confusion about Dr Kader. At the time, on the plane, Eva had been so angry to see Xavier's godfather, she'd even drawn a gun on him.

Who could blame me? Last I heard, he betrayed Sam in Denver.

But Dr Dark had explained that Ahmed had been working for them all along, winning Mac's trust and finding out what he knew.

And Dr Dark wouldn't welcome a traitor back. He must have been a spy for Dr Dark and the Academy all along.

Eva let out a sigh and rolled out of bed. Thinking about who they could trust, who was on whose side, only made her mind race even more. She figured if she was going to be awake, she might as well use the time to do something.

Maybe then I'll feel like sleeping . . .

She changed from her pyjamas to her Stealth Suit and tiptoed out of the room and down the hallway.

Outside the dorm building she ran through the crisp night, the moon and stars hidden by low clouds. She knew that a large contingent of the Guardians protecting the Academy's London campus would be patrolling the grounds and buildings, and wouldn't be happy to find her sneaking around so late. She moved quickly and silently across the dewy grass to visit her friend.

Jedi's lab was underneath the boathouse, and as Eva crept down the stairs, she smiled. He was playing music, which meant that he was still wide-awake and probably working.

'Hey, Eva,' Jedi said, not even turning around in his high-backed chair to see that it was her.

'How did you . . . how'd you know it was me?' Eva asked.

'This,' he said.

Eva stood by his side, and he was pointing at one of several large screens on his desk. Each screen was divided into several sections, each showing a different place around the campus.

'New advanced security system. The campus CCTV cameras are tiny—completely unnoticeable,' Jedi explained. 'Seems like we're not the only ones who can't sleep. Sam's currently in the dojo,' he continued, pointing to a square on one screen. 'And over here, we can see that the Professor's still working in his study—he likes to pace back and forth when he's thinking. And six students, here,' he tapped another screen, 'seem to be having a bit of a party in their common room.'

'Looks like there's a lot of insomnia going around. Huh,' Eva muttered.

Jedi tapped a few keys and the screens changed, now showing hundreds of dots scattered over a graphic. The graphic was divided by wavy lines criss-crossing one another. When Jedi tapped on a particular dot, a student's name appeared, along with other numerical data.

'What's that?'

'The dreamwaves on the campus. Kinda like our own mini Dreamscape.'

'Everyone's dreamwaves are being read via these?' Eva asked, holding her dreamcatcher.

'Yep,' Jedi replied, 'Nifty, huh?'

'What's with the different colours of the dots?'

'Ah, OK, look here,' Jedi said, pointing to a cluster in the senior wing of the dorm. 'See the aura colours of their dream states?'

Eva looked at the colours. They were dark red, a couple almost black.

'They're asleep,' Jedi said, 'and they're having nightmares. Bad ones, by the colour coding. It's similar to what I see when we've done recent scans of a wider area Dreamscape—towns and cities at night—the general populace can't control or steer dreams at all, so they're having terrible nightmares.'

'What do the last 13 Dreamers look like when they sleep?'

Jedi smiled and brought up the schematic diagrams of the dots labelled: Zara, Gabriella, Xavier, Rapha, Maria, Cody and Arianna. Their dream colours were a cool white-blue, reminding Eva of the summer skies over her home town of Seattle.

'Identical,' Eva noticed.

'They are—here,' Jedi said.

'What do you mean?' Eva asked.

'Aural spectrums can be influenced by certain factors. In this case, it's the Gears. Of course, we are researching this more as we go, but from looking at the last 13 Dreamers, we got lucky and realised that their aura colours and dreamwave patterns become the same when they're dreaming close to a Gear.'

Jedi called up recorded data to show her.

'Cool.'

Jedi made a few adjustments and little graphs came up next to each of the last 13. 'And this shows in greater detail the colours and what they represent, as well as the sleep patterns, length of REM sleep, whether they're in a lucid dream, that kind of thing,' Jedi said. 'It gives an overall number that we call a Dream Aura Count. See here?'

He zoomed in.

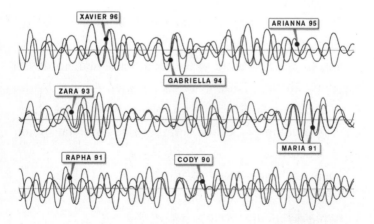

'They're all in the nineties,' Eva said. 'Is that good?'

'Yep. Only the Professor gets close to that and he's at about eighty-three or eighty-four. Lora's at seventy-five, Tobias too. Most teachers, including me, are in the high sixties.'

'Students?'

'Well, the base worldwide population is anywhere between one and ten, so when juniors arrive at the Academy they are not much above that, usually in the twenties. And the highest senior we ever had graduated at sixty-five, and that was Lora.'

'Wow.'

'There was only one other who came close to her Dream Aura Count,' Jedi said, leaning back in his chair, staring up at the ceiling, his hands cupped behind his head. 'Yeah . . . according to the data I inherited, Sebastian's count was abnormally high too.'

'Well, I guess he'd have a natural advantage being the Professor's son, huh?'

Jedi nodded. 'What a waste to lose someone so gifted— especially now.'

Eva paused, not quite knowing what to say next. After a long moment she asked, 'So, what does my aura look like at night?'

'Oh, yours is the same,' Jedi replied casually.

'What?'

Same as . . . does he mean . . ?

Jedi clicked through several screens and opened a file, bringing up Eva's archived dream data.

Eva stared. 'But how . . ? Hang on, it says there that my Dream Aura Count is in the nineties too . . .'

Jedi smiled. 'Mm-hmm.'

'But, that would mean . . . what are you saying exactly?' Eva's heart started thudding in her chest and she could feel blood rushing to her face.

'It means . . .' Jedi said, touching the screen to zoom in on her data as a loud beep rang out, making Eva jump. Jedi hurriedly turned back to the first screen, frantically tapping away at his keyboard. 'Oh . . . oh no, you don't . . .'

'Jedi? What is it?'

'My system,' Jedi said, rolling cross the floor to another terminal and punching in commands. 'It's another hacking attempt!'

'Matrix?'

'Yep.'

'Can I help?'

'Yeah, actually you can. Get on that console there,' he said, pointing, 'and do exactly what I say!'

SAM

Sam couldn't sleep. Not even after a midnight training session.

After dinner he'd had a haircut—a short buzz cut, thanks to one of the senior boys—and gotten himself a new generation Stealth Suit, specially provided for him by the tech-heads in the Advance Science department at the Enterprise. According to them, this new Suit could function in a sub-zero environment and had enough power to last twenty-four hours whilst completely immobile. Then it would need at least an hour's worth of constant motion or body warmth to recharge.

Never want to test that particular limit.

Now it resembled casual gym wear as he rested in his bedroom. The room was small but it felt safe. Where there had once been Academy merchandise in this would-be storeroom, there was now a single bed, a small desk, a wardrobe and bookshelves. The old sash window had heavy curtains to keep out the London winters.

Sam sat at the desk and stared outside. In the midnight shadows of the moon, he made out teams of Guardians patrolling the grounds, serious-looking people with serious-looking guns.

He stood up and moved across the small room to sit on his bed. His bedside lamp remained on, and he sat there, motionless.

Waiting.

For what?

He did not feel sleepy at all.

So what now? Am I just going to sit here, waiting, until dawn breaks?

He picked up a book and opened it. It was something about Egyptian gods. He was leafing through the pages but not taking anything in.

Unease was setting in. Sleep was definitely a long way off now. He decided to head back down to the dojo to spend another hour working on his throwing and grappling moves.

He took the spiral staircase all the way down to the basement gymnasium where the combat classes were held. He went through his warm-up routine of five minutes on the skipping rope, a series of stretches and fifty push-ups.

He got a sparring dummy out of the equipment room.

Over the next half hour, he worked through a series of throws, escapes, take downs, reversals and joint locks. He worked, moving fast and furiously, stopping only when his body ached and he felt as though he could now have a shower and sleep soundly.

'You're pretty handy against an opponent who can't fight back,' a voice said.

Sam spun around, alarmed, searching the shadows.

Stepping from the darkness at the end of the stairs, a familiar figure emerged. He had a scruffy beard and dishevelled hair, and he was the most welcome sight Sam could imagine.

'Tobias!' Sam said, running over to hug his old teacher and friend. 'Where have you been?'

'Here and there,' Tobias said.

'He was on a mission for me . . .' the Professor said, entering the room. 'And he's back to embark on another.'

'Another?' Sam said, his voice crestfallen. 'You have to go again?'

'Yes,' Tobias said, 'with you.'

'Really?'

'Yes,' Tobias said. 'Change of plans. We're leaving now, under the cover of darkness, to head for Japan.'

'Where's Lora? Is she ready?'

'Sam, we think it would be best if we changed the details of your dream,' the Professor said. 'Instead of travelling with you to Japan, Lora will remain here. There are important preparations to make before the Four Corners Competition. Tobias will now accompany you—he has contacts in Japan.'

'So we run away during the night?' Sam said. He looked from Tobias to the Professor, seeing that the decision had already been made. 'Does Lora even know?'

'No.' The Professor looked pained as he spoke. 'Sam, you are always being cornered and captured wherever you go by enemies who seem to be aware of our plans,' the Professor said. 'We need to take every precaution we can—even here.'

'You're not suggesting Lora is . . .'

'Of course not,' Tobias said. 'We just need to change things up. It can't hurt to catch everyone by surprise, even if that includes a few of our own people.'

'OK,' Sam said, seeing sense in the plan, but still feeling somewhat disloyal to Lora. 'How soon do we leave?'

Tobias grinned and handed Sam his backpack, which Sam had packed hours earlier and left by his room door in readiness. 'Now.'

'Can I say goodbye to the others?'

Tobias chuckled and said, 'That kind of defeats the purpose of us slipping off secretly, don't you think?'

'Oh, right . . .' Sam said. He changed his Stealth Suit's appearance from the jujitsu outfit into dark-coloured street clothes. The three of them climbed the stairs and stopped outside the main doors of the gymnasium. Four Guardians stood, guns drawn, next to two sleek sports cars.

'Our ride to the airport,' Tobias explained.

'Nice,' Sam said.

'Goodbye, Sam, until next time.' The Professor shook Sam's hand and then pointed to Sam's hair. 'This all the rage these days?'

'Ah, yeah, you could say that,' Sam said.

'Well, you be careful out there,' the Professor said. 'And stay close to Tobias.'

'Will do,' Sam said as he headed for the nearest car. He stopped and turned around. 'Oh, one more thing, Professor? What's the championship you mentioned?'

'That, Sam,' the Professor said, 'is probably the only chance we have of finding the Gears that Solaris has taken from us.'

Sam boarded the Boeing 787 with Tobias. They were directed to their seats in economy class.

'No private jet this time, huh?' Sam said, buckling in. When he looked across at Tobias he laughed—his disguise was hilarious. Tobias was wearing a thick moustache, large square glasses, and his Stealth Suit was transformed into an old-fashioned brown suit.

'Just blending in with the masses, Master Hawks,' Tobias said, referring to Sam's false name on his false passport—John Hawks. Tobias' own passport was in the name of Peter Hawks, John's uncle, Tobias had explained.

'Blending in?' Sam laughed. 'With what decade?'

Tobias rolled his eyes and pretended to take offence.

'And when we touch down in Tokyo?' Sam asked, this time in a whisper.

'We'll go to the gaming tournament to find Issey,' Tobias replied quietly. 'It's on tonight, and we're on the guest list.'

'Of course we are,' Sam said. 'But I won't need to convince Issey that he's a Dreamer and part of the prophecy?'

'No, not this time. Well, not completely,' Tobias replied,

as the aircraft began taxiing to the runway. 'Issey's Enterprise parents have been quite open about who they are, much like Cody's parents were with him.'

'Open? I didn't think the Enterprise would allow that, you know, especially with how they used to be at the start of all this.' Sam thought of his own surrogate parents.

'Well, I don't think it was the recommended course of action, but it doesn't seem to have been forbidden. In any case, Issey knows all about Dreamers and true dreams. Although his parents have not been informed by us that he's one of the last 13. We couldn't risk alerting them ahead of time just in case. That will be down to you.'

'Well, it's an advantage not to have to start at the very beginning,' Sam said, tightening his belt for take-off. 'I found that out with Arianna. I wonder how Issey will take it?'

'Oh, something tells me he's going to take it just fine.'

Sam sat back in silence as the aircraft took off, the force pushing him back in his seat. He was tired now, his eyes heavy, finally wanting to sleep.

Sam startled.

'Sam?'

He looked across to Tobias, who had his reading light on and was sitting there next to him with a book open and a cup of coffee curling steam around them. The window shade was half-open and the sun shone brightly outside.

Sam stretched out, yawning. He still felt wrecked. 'How long was I out?'

'For a few hours.'

'I was so tired. Still am . . .' Sam looked about the dimly lit cabin. Most of the other window blinds were down and nearly everyone was still asleep. 'I was just thinking back. I was watching a scene play back, just like when Jedi records it. Reliving it. That's happened before.'

'That's how your dreaming works, when you're steering it,' Tobias replied, sipping his coffee. 'You're learning, even without lessons.'

'But—I wasn't steering anything,' Sam said. 'I was just thinking back to when I was in Russia, a tiny moment.'

'You went back and saw things from a different perspective,' Tobias replied. 'Soon you'll be doing that more and more—just as you have your dreams of the last 13 that turn out to be real, after this race you will have everyday dreams where you are able to see things from any vantage point, well before they actually happen.'

Sam nodded, rubbing the sleep from his eyes and clearing his mind. He pressed the call button for the flight attendant. A friendly man in a crisp uniform came quickly. 'A coffee please, and maybe some biscuits?'

The attendant nodded and left.

'I'm done with sleep for a while,' Sam said to Tobias, who chuckled and folded away his glasses and book.

'Fine,' Tobias replied. 'Then I will teach you what I know about Dream Steering for the next few hours. But be warned, just like my science classes back at school, you may just be bored back to sleep.'

They chuckled and Sam listened as his old teacher spoke of dreams and Dreamers who had achieved so much, and the art and science of steering dreams.

Sam and Tobias drove through the streets of Tokyo in a hire car.

Tobias looked anxious. Jedi had sent a message saying that Stella's Agents had been seen in Japan. 'It would seem that our stealthy departure was not as effective as we would have hoped it to be,' he said.

'At least we have people watching over Issey, though,' Sam said.

'True, the Guardians following him are good,' Tobias said. 'But they're still only twelve people.'

'How does Stella always seem to know? No matter what we do?' Sam asked, exasperated.

Tobias shrugged. Sam could tell by his distant look that he was turning the question over in his head.

'So what's our plan?' Sam asked after a while.

'Same as before. We go to the tournament and we get Issey out.'

'And if it's not that easy?'

'Well, let's hope it is. Then again, if it was easy, there'd be no fun in it, right?'

'Yeah, I know,' Sam said laughing at his attempt to lighten the mood. 'But seriously though, how am I going to get him to just walk away from such a big moment? Not to mention the million-dollar prize and the sports car.'

'For Issey, it's all a game,' Tobias said, slowing the car as the traffic began to bank-up on the highway. 'He's been aware of Dreamers his whole life. He'll understand what you're telling him. It's just making him understand the urgency.'

'Yeah, we'll see,' Sam said, watching the bright lights of the big city all around. 'And you're sure we can't just call the Guardians to get him out?'

'No. If Stella's men are on the move, it's better if the Guardians are watching out for that,' Tobias said.

'OK,' Sam said, watching Tokyo flit past outside the window, all lights and ads and people everywhere. 'Aren't you tired?'

'I'll sleep well when all this is over,' Tobias said. 'I've been tired for years, why worry about it now?'

There was a long silence. 'I don't like the idea of failure,' Sam admitted, absently gazing at the tall buildings as they drove by. 'All that could go wrong. If I fail today, or tomorrow—or at the end.'

'Focus on what can go *right*, and what you can do in this moment,' Tobias said. 'If we let the possibility of failure stop us from even trying, then nothing would ever get achieved.'

'Yeah, I know . . .'

'Self-doubt is normal, Sam, and in some ways it can be a good thing,' Tobias said. 'It keeps it real—isn't that what you kids say?'

Sam laughed. 'No, I don't think we do! But I know you're right,' he said.

ALEX

Alex and Shiva had rested, neither sleeping soundly. Alex woke first and looked at his wrist in a panic, but the wrist bomb was just as they'd left it, the cover off, the anti-tamper mechanism re-routed with wire, the red and blue wires from the detonator to the explosive still there, taunting them.

Great.

Alex stood up. 'OK, OK, we *have* to do this, so let's do it.'

Shiva snorted awake. 'Excellent. OK, I'm ready. Get the clippers.'

'Here,' Alex said, passing them over and pacing on the spot, shifting his weight from foot to foot as he worked up the courage. 'So, we said cut the blue wire, right? We're agreed on that?'

'I'm pretty sure we said red,' Shiva said, the clippers open in his hand.

'What? No, like ages ago, we talked about it, right? We agreed blue.'

'Ages ago I wasn't captive in an unknown apartment, imprisoned by my former boss who's since turned into an arch criminal hell-bent on taking over the Dreamscape.'

Alex swallowed hard and nodded. 'OK, fine, but not *that* ages ago. But, ah . . . hey, wait—why are we doing this to *my* wristband?'

'Huh?'

'Yeah, I mean, why can't we start with yours?' Alex said.

'Because . . . I can't remember,' Shiva said. 'But we already spent a few hours disassembling yours and pulling out the wiring, so let's stick to the plan, OK?'

'OK. Wait—we had a plan?'

'Yeah, the blue wire,' Shiva replied.

'Right. No, you said red before!' Alex said.

'Blue, I meant blue. You said blue, we agreed on blue. Ages ago. Right?'

'Right. I mean, I—I don't know. Maybe we should wait?' Alex faltered.

'Good idea. But wait for what, Christmas?' Shiva said. 'For the battery in the mechanism to conk out?'

'Will it?' Alex was hopeful.

'Sure. Might take a year or two, though, like a watch battery,' Shiva replied.

'Oh.' Alex looked around the bare apartment. 'Hey, you know what, how about a drinks break? Yeah? Maybe a snack?'

'Relax, Alex. We'll get this, no problem. One wire, one cut.'

'What if it's the wrong wire?'

'Then the timer will start.'

'A five-minute countdown?' Alex asked.

'Five minutes,' Shiva said.

'Then boom?'

'Then boom.'

'Great, just great.' Alex wiped sweat from his forehead. 'Then we could just cut the other?'

'No. That would detonate it immediately,' Shiva said.

'Oh, right.'

Shiva shifted, raising the clippers. 'OK, man, I'm cutting—'

'Wait!'

'What?'

Alex sat down next to Shiva, his face pained, his breathing short and sharp.

'We *do* need a plan,' he said. 'We got it this far, now let's plan. If we cut the wrong wire, the timer starts. We need a plan B for that. Like, think about it—where do we go?'

'To Matrix. He's got the reset code.'

'Right. How on earth do we find him?' Alex asked. 'He could be anywhere!'

'I bet I know just where he is,' Shiva smiled.

'You do?' Alex asked.

'Yep, he's got a secret workshop and he'd need his equipment to work on the Coils so it makes sense that he'd move them there,' Shiva said.

'Great. Where's that?'

'It's a disused subway station, downtown, in the financial district. He doesn't know I know about it but I came across it in his files once. You know, when I was *browsing* . . .'

'You're sure?'

'Yep, it's actually perfect. There's still power from the subway grid running through it, which he'll need for the Coils.'

'How far away is it?' Alex asked.

Shiva attempted to calculate their current location from the tiny speck they could see of the blacked-out window—a sliver of Central Park.

'My guess would be about sixty blocks south,' Shiva said.

'Right,' Alex said. 'Good. So plan B is that we go to him.'

'In under five minutes,' Shiva said, his voice downbeat.

'Is that not doable?' Alex hesitated.

'Have you got a magic carpet? Or, better yet, a teleportation device?'

'Hmm, let me check,' Alex stood and made a show of patting down his pockets. 'Should be somewhere here . . . nup, you know what, I'm all out of those.'

'Shame. Never around when you need them, right?'

'Right. Let's see . . . something fast. What about a cop car?'

'Sixty blocks south in any car in Manhattan? Take a while. Longer than five minutes.'

'It's well after rush hour,' Alex said, looking out the

window's peek hole and seeing a bright day. 'And we could use the siren.'

'Even running every red light we'd hit a jam someplace. Cop car's no good. How'd we steal one of those anyway?'

'Right, forget that . . .' Alex sat back down. Then, panic spread over his face.

'What is it?' Shiva asked.

Alex's face pinched, his eyes closing tight.

Then he sneezed.

A huge, violent sneeze. His whole body shook with the force.

They looked down at the wristband. A wire had come loose from the timer mechanism.

The red wire.

The device did not explode.

'Sweet!'

'No . . .' Shiva said, turning over the face of the wristband.

The face showed the countdown had begun.

4:59

4:58

4:57

SAM

The tournament arena was exactly as Sam dreamed it, right down to the paparazzi pushing and shoving with camera flashes popping every second.

Sam waited nervously for Issey and his entourage to arrive. When the limo car door swung open and Issey stepped out, he wore his best media smile but his eyes were searching, sweeping the faces in the crowd. Sam waved to him, hopelessly lost in the throng, but as soon as Issey saw him, there was a flash of recognition in his eyes. He turned to his assistant and within moments, Sam was waved through and found himself on the red carpet.

'Issey, I'm Sam,' Sam said, thrusting out his hand.

Issey clasped his hand and whispered in his ear, 'I've been expecting you, Sam. It's amazing to meet you. Now, smile for the cameras!'

Issey navigated the photographers with well-practised ease and soon they were safely inside the roped-off area and able to speak freely.

When Sam explained to Issey about why he'd come, Issey took it as well as Tobias had predicted.

'No way! I dreamed of you, Sam, but I didn't know what that meant. Me? Part of the prophecy!' Issey exclaimed.

'It's true,' Sam said.

'No way! Like, *no way!*'

'Well, yes, way,' Sam said.

Issey jumped up into the air in excitement. '*Sugoi!* I mean, how cool is *that?*'

'It's pretty cool,' Sam said. 'Though perhaps not quite as much as you're thinking it is. It's quite dangerous—'

'I love danger!' He turned around, and pointed with his thumbs over his shoulders to the back of his leather jacket. It read:

TEAM DANGER

'Yeah, I don't think you're quite getting the level of danger that I mean,' Sam said, and he opened his jacket to reveal the grip of the dark pistol tucked into his belt.

'Awesome! Is that, like, real?'

'Yes—'

'Can I have one?'

'Well, maybe, but like I said, this thing we have to do, it's quite dangerous—'

'I love danger!'

What is this guy on?

'Oh, man!' Issey went on. 'This is the coolest night of my life.'

The crowd went nuts as the lights dimmed.

'See you after the tournament!' Issey waved to the

crowd and strutted to his place.

Sam walked back to his front row seat next to Tobias.

'How'd he take it?' Tobias asked.

'Well, OK, but I'm not sure he's really grasping the situation. It's like he's so successful that he thinks he's invincible,' Sam replied. 'Man, if I ever get a big head like that . . . I don't know, but do something, don't let me get away with it.'

'Sure will,' Tobias said cheerily.

They were silent for a moment.

'Do you think he'll show?' Sam said, scanning the crowd.

'Solaris?'

'Yeah,' Sam replied.

'Don't know. Jedi tried to track the escape pods out from Denver, but with no luck. We know he's out there, somewhere. We just have to be extra careful.'

'Like sneaking out on Lora?' Sam asked. 'It didn't work though. Stella is still in town . . .'

Tobias took a heavy breath. 'I just think that it's best if we work in the dark as much as possible. The less people who know your movements, the better.'

EVA

In the morning, Eva went looking for Sam and Lora and could not find either of them. She headed for the Professor's office, but as she walked up to the door, she stopped.

Eva could hear yelling. She put her ear to the door and quickly realised from the conversation happening inside that Sam had left in the night with Tobias.

'Why would you keep me in the dark on this?' Lora demanded.

'Lora, I am sorry,' the Professor said, 'but we had to keep this quiet.'

'You don't trust me?'

'I do trust you, you know that.'

'Then why didn't you tell me? Why the secrecy?'

'Because there was no time.'

'There was time to at least keep me in the loop—I oversee all the operations here.'

'Ah . . .' the Professor sighed. 'Yes, you're right. I'm sorry.'

'Well, I'm not happy about this. I think it's wrong, and

dangerous. We know Stella has been sighted in Japan.'

Eva heard footsteps nearing and shuffled from the door to behind the sofa in the waiting room in case Lora stormed out. From the open window behind her, she could still hear the conversation from the Professor's open office window further along the wall.

'I know, Lora, I know. But it was all in good faith,' the Professor said. 'I have fears, grave fears, that someone can see into our dreams—*all* our dreams.'

There was silence, and Eva leaned out the window a little to hear.

'I worried that if you or Sam slept last night,' the Professor said, 'or me, for that matter, that our travel plans might have been seen.'

There was more silence.

Lora's weighing up what the Professor is saying. What are they talking about?

'And if something happens to Sam?' Lora said finally.

'There's always that risk, you know that,' the Professor replied. 'But he's with Tobias, and there are Guardians there too. They'll be careful.'

Sam's gone?

'Stella's force could be ten times the number of Guardians,' Lora countered. 'And Hans and Solaris are still out there somewhere.'

'Lora, please. I need you here, we *all* do,' the Professor said. 'You must get the Dreamer Doors team ready. They can help us find the missing Gears. Isn't that what you told me?'

'Yes—yes I know, you're right,' Lora said. 'But Sam is more important than anything else right now.'

'I know, but this is vital too.'

'I understand we must find the Gears that have fallen into other hands, but . . .' There was a pause, then Lora went on, 'But there's something else to it, isn't there? Something else that you've yet to tell me.'

'Yes.'

'What?'

'Lora, hopefully running the competition will help counter some of the nightmares the world is experiencing at the moment, and in turn that could save countless lives,' the Professor said. 'And it will buy us time.'

There was silence then and when Lora next spoke her voice was calm and reconciled.

'OK,' she said, 'I'll work on the selection.'

Eva ducked down as Lora left the Professor's office and Eva waited, hidden in silence, hearing her walk away.

'Eva, you can come in now,' the Professor called out.

Eva abruptly stood up and looked around to find the hidden camera.

Jedi!

She went into the Professor's office, looking sheepish. She found him standing there, smiling.

'You're worried about Sam,' he said. 'But he'll be fine.'

'How are you so sure?' Eva asked.

'Because you dreamed it, last night,' the Professor said. 'And just like you dreamed of that helicopter ride that you and Sam and Alex took a few weeks back, that dream will come true too.'

'You're right. I . . . I dreamed of Sam, and we were somewhere hot, like a desert. But then you know that, because you've seen it, haven't you?'

'Yes,' the Professor said, bringing her recorded dream up on a screen in the room. 'And I had Jedi map the stars that are visible in the sky.'

'Oh?'

'From their positioning, we can work out that this event happens a couple of weeks from now.'

'So Sam will be OK . . .'

'For now, that appears to be the case.'

'But the future can change,' Eva said. 'You've said so, I've read about it. Tobias leaving with Sam instead of Lora, as in Sam's dream—that's already changing the future.'

'Yes, the more we change things like that, the more it changes what's going to happen,' the Professor agreed.

'That's what scares me,' Eva said.

SAM

'We need to get out of here,' Sam said, looking around at the lights of the arena.

'Tonight is the semi-final,' Tobias said. 'We've changed your dream, which had us here tomorrow at the final.'

'So we're a day ahead,' Sam said, still scanning the scene. They were seated near the floor and all around the crowds had on t-shirts emblazoned with either Issey's red team or the Hong Kong green team. Red and green glowsticks punctuated the air around them. The house lights went down, making it hard to really see the crowd but for the colours they wore. Powerful spotlights and strobes roamed across the arena, while laser lighting made fast-moving patterns all around the ceiling. 'Still, I don't know . . . this feels spooky.'

'We'll talk to Issey again once he's done his thing,' Tobias said, 'then we'll get out of Tokyo fast and see where we need to go for his Gear.'

'But we'll have to convince him to miss the final tournament tomorrow,' Sam said, shifting in his seat as his dart pistol dug into the small of his back where he'd tucked it into his Stealth Suit. 'And what if they change things up too? Stella or whoever, or *whatever*, gets in here, not tomorrow, but tonight?'

'All the entry-points are being watched by Guardians, so we'll have warning.'

'Yeah, I guess,' Sam said, looking around uneasily.

What were those beasts from my dream? They can't be real, right?

Sam saw on the giant screen that Issey was entering the fifth and deciding round to win the night's tournament and advance to the final. The home crowd was skewed in his favour, but the Hong Kong contingent was making up for their smaller number with a rapturous cheer squad.

'How much longer do you think?' Sam asked.

'The way Issey demolished the guy in that last heat,' Tobias said, leaning forward and watching a huge screen showing the tactics being used by both players in the monster-fighting game, 'I think it'll be over soo—'

All of a sudden the power went out. All the lighting, gone. The computers and jumbo screens. Everything was in complete darkness.

Sam tensed. All around them, the raised glowsticks went still.

'Tobias—my dream.'

'I know, stay close.'

They both drew their dart pistols.

'Those beasts from my dream—'

'They were just a manifestation,' Tobias said, his voice calm. 'They symbolise your enemy. It's what your dreaming mind does when searching for answers and projecting fears. Whoever is here, rest assured they're human.'

Then the screaming started.

The emergency generators kicked in, casting a dim glow over the seething masses of people as they desperately made for the exits in fear.

Sam started to shake.

'Sam, keep cool, OK?' Tobias said. 'Let's get down to Issey. The Guardians will move in from the exits to help us get out.'

The screams intensified to the left of them. Glowsticks were moving fast—away from something.

Then, thin blue laser lights pierced the gloom, dozens of them, emerging from the four main entry points.

'Ah,' Tobias said. 'I'd say Stella and her thugs have crashed the party.'

'Where was our Guardian warning?'

'I don't know.'

'What are the laser pointers they're using?'

'They're using low-light optics and laser-aiming on their dart rifles. Follow me.'

Sam followed close behind Tobias, who was talking into his phone's mic. They rushed to Issey on stage.

'Sam, you and Issey go out through the south exit, there,' Tobias pointed across the room.

'But the Agents—'

'The Guardians were called to the south by a fake distress call,' Tobias said. 'They're coming in behind her force there now, they'll blast you a hole to escape.'

'What about you?' Sam said.

'I'm going to create a diversion,' Tobias said. 'Here, take a couple of these.'

He passed Sam three heavy objects, the size of table-tennis balls, with a tiny switch on each.

'Smoke screens,' Tobias said, switching on a couple and tossing them. 'Now go, run, and I'll contact you outside once we're all clear!'

WHACK!

Sam shot a rogue Agent in the chest.

WHACK!

And another.

'Can I have one of those?' Issey asked, pointing to Sam's dart gun, but Sam didn't have time to answer. The stairwell to the south erupted with twelve Guardians, each of the hulking soldiers taking expert aim at the traitorous Agents and dispatching them, surprise on their side.

'Issey, follow me!' Sam said, heading for the safety cordon that the Guardians had formed. 'Run!'

ALEX

'You want the good news or the bad news first?' Shiva asked.

'*What?*'

Alex checked the countdown.

4:34

The lift to the lobby had taken twenty seconds. They now stood in the middle of a bustling city street. After a week of being cooped up in the apartment, the bright sunshine and noise of life around them was almost overwhelming.

'OK, the bad news is we're further away than I thought,' Shiva said.

'And the good?!'

'We've got a flying carpet to get us there!' Shiva said. He ran to a courier's motorbike, the engine idling, its owner obviously inside one of the corporate buildings nearby, distracted with an urgent delivery. 'Get on!'

Alex didn't need to be told twice.

Shiva threw the bike into gear and dropped the clutch, gunning the throttle as they burned a circle of rubber and took off down the street. Alex looked back just in time to see an angry courier standing in the middle of the road, shouting and pulling out a phone.

That's all we need—more cops after us!

Alex couldn't stop checking the countdown on the display.

4:29

Shiva took a hard right turn at the next intersection, steering frantically between cars, then weaving around a line of cabs, taking the oncoming lane which was largely deserted.

4:11

Come on, come on!

Five blocks down, Alex chose a new mantra.

We're gonna make it. We're gonna make it.

The light ahead was red. Cars and trucks began to travel across the intersection as their traffic lane slowed down.

We're not going to make it!

Shiva didn't slow down. He sped up, opening the throttle the whole way. They flashed through the intersection, scraping between a truck and car.

Alex closed his eyes. He heard horns blare and tyres screech.

Shiva whooped in victory, the bike wobbling danger-ously as he pumped the air.

Alex looked back.

Two cars had swerved to avoid hitting them, colliding with one another in an awful-sounding smash. Both drivers had their doors open fast, looking down the road at the bike, shaking their fists in rage.

Shiva didn't bother looking back. He just kept on riding, speeding ahead, taking them south, towards where he thought Matrix would be.

Alex checked his wristband.

3:52

We will make it—

Shiva slammed on the brakes.

The bike was shrouded in smoke from burning rubber as the locked-up wheels kept careening them forward.

Oh no!

The intersection at 31st Street was a traffic jam and a cab door opened right in front of them, blocking off the space Shiva had been aiming for.

Shiva downshifted gears, keeping the brakes locked, revving the engine.

But it was too late.

We're gonna crash!

They hit the taxi door and both of them catapulted from the bike, flying through the air.

SAM

Outside the stadium, Sam and Issey ran in among the stream of thousands of spectators.

'We need to get in a car!' Sam said.

'This way!' Issey replied, peeling off from the main crowd and heading for a building.

'Issey, we need a *car*, not cover!' Sam said, but he went unheard because Issey was fast—*very* fast. Sam sprinted across the street and down a car park ramp and came to a level full of cars—and no people.

'Issey?' Sam called.

I'm sure he ran down here . . .

He turned around and around but could see no-one. 'Issey!'

VROOM!

'Argh!' Sam jumped out of the way as a bright yellow sports car screeched up behind him.

Issey was at the wheel.

'Get in!' Issey yelled.

Sam did.

And regretted it almost at once.

'Issssssseeeeeeey!' Sam said, his face plastered to the inside of the passenger window as Issey did a handbrake turn outside the car park and roared up the street at warp speed. 'This is scarier than being back there in the arena!' Sam muttered.

'Hang on!' Issey said, pulling on the brake again and turning in a cloud of tyre smoke. He hit the accelerator and they were moving at light speed once more, this time down the wrong way of a one-way street.

'Issey, you don't have to drive like a madman!' Sam said. 'We just need to get some distance between us and them.'

'Oh, there's a rush,' Issey replied. 'Look behind us.'

Sam turned around in the seat, steadying himself as Issey flipped the steering wheel to slide them out onto a new street.

Behind, two other cars made the same turns.

'Right,' Sam said. He wound down the window, pressed a button on a smoke bomb, and tossed it out.

He watched for the result, which was almost instant.

BANG!

The smoke erupted into a thick cloud, forming a wall across the street.

But both pursuing cars punched through it, not even slowing for a second.

'Damn,' Sam said, buckling up and looking to Issey. 'OK, do it your way, shake them.'

'On it!' Issey replied, stomping on the brakes.

Their car screeched to a sudden stop.

'You're *stopping?*' Sam said, then saw the sense of the plan.

Both the pursuing cars flashed by, surprised by the move and braking too late. Too late, because Issey was already reversing—fast.

It's like he's in a game and he's thinking several steps ahead.

'Isseeeey!' Sam said as Issey was in motion with another move—several in fact. He pulled the handbrake and flicked the steering wheel, turning the car on the spot and speeding them down the road, taking two quick turns and then flooring it. Sam looked behind. Stella's cars were nowhere to be seen—yet.

'Nice driving!' Sam said, working out a crick in his neck. 'Where'd you learn all this?'

'On a console.'

'You're not serious?' Sam laughed.

'Yep.'

'But you have a licence, right?'

'How old do you think I am?' Issey grinned.

'Uh-oh. Then whose car is this?'

'Somebody's,' Issey replied.

'Huh?'

'I boosted it.'

'What?' Sam shook his head.

'I took the keys from the attendant's booth,' Issey said. 'My parents park their car there, and you have to leave the keys. The old guy's always falling asleep, and I've seen this car there before . . . hang on.'

Sam grabbed hold of the dashboard in front of him as Issey pulled the brake and drifted onto a side road, releasing the brake to shoot down the street in one smooth motion.

Issey looked to Sam and smiled. 'What?' he said.

'I—nothing,' Sam said, hanging on for grim life as Issey navigated them via another drift onto a highway on-ramp, taking them up onto an elevated road. He looked out the rear window. There were no cars following them now. 'Just head someplace safe, preferably in one piece.'

'Will do,' Issey said, then his demeanour changed.

'What?' Sam asked, his anxiety immediately back.

'We've got a new tail,' Issey replied, motioning to his side mirror.

Sam turned around again for another look. It was the car from the tournament, the prize car, closing in fast. Before Issey could react, it rammed their back bumper, and in that moment, Sam could make out the driver—*Stella!*

'Oh man . . .'

'Who is it?' Issey asked as he sped up, but the car behind was gaining.

'She's called Stella. And she's bad news, the worst. Can you lose her?'

'My foot's flat to the floor whenever I have the chance,' Issey said, weaving in and out of the other cars on the road.

'We need another plan,' Sam said, watching as Stella mirrored their every move.

'I may have one,' Issey replied.

Sam looked ahead. There was a roadwork sign at an exit ramp, and then another.

'Oh no, you're not!' Sam said, holding onto the dashboard as Issey steered towards the exit.

'She'd be crazy to follow us!' Issey replied, smashing through the signs. Both front airbags deployed but Issey didn't miss a beat.

Sam frantically tried to deflate them as he looked over the back of his seat. Stella was still coming hard behind them.

'Forgot to mention,' Sam said, winding his window down to let out the white powdery dust from the airbags, 'she's crazy!'

'Well, hang on to your . . . something!'

Sam looked ahead. There was no *road* ahead. The sports

car's big engine was roaring. They were getting ahead of Stella now there were no other cars on the road.

'What the . . ?' Sam looked out his side window. He could see a grassed park below, with a pond and maple trees that swept their branches down to the water.

And no more road.

Out in front he saw—a whole section was yet to be built.

'Oh, damn!' Issey said.

'Are you joking?' Sam yelled.

'I thought we'd make it!'

'Issey! Stop!!' Sam closed his eyes.

'Brace!'

EVA

As Eva finished watching the replay from the previous year's Dreamer Doors final, she eased off the 3-D viewing visor. It took a while for her eyes to adjust to the light of the Professor's office. The Professor was pouring a cup of coffee and sitting behind his desk, papers scattered everywhere around him.

'Well?' he asked.

'It . . . it was strange,' Eva replied.

'It always is, watching the dream from the point of view of the Dreamer,' he said. 'Unlike those you have seen replayed before on screens, where it is as if we are observing the action, in this case, you are a participant— you see what those Dreamers saw.'

'And I'm not sure what they saw,' Eva sighed.

The Professor leaned back, the coffee cup in his hands, steam rising before his face.

'When you watch the dream from the Dreamer's point of view,' he said, 'you see the world as they do, and that includes details that, to the untrained, only make sense to the Dreamer.'

'Such as the flying house?' Eva said.

'Exactly. Surely there is no actual flying house, but that is what that student saw—he and his team, in a house, flying through the sky. To him it was as real as us sitting here now.'

'So things that couldn't possibly be in the real world, can feel real in the competition?'

'Yes, these things manifest as if they are real. So, more than ever, knowing the difference between reality and what is dreamed, is crucial when competing in the Dreamer Doors.'

'Right—so where our true dreams are grounded in reality, in this competition, the dream could really be anything and anywhere?'

'Correct. It's really up to the individual Dreamer whose dream the competition will be held in.'

'But there was something else—I saw blood on his hands,' Eva said.

'Yes, but after that we see that he and his teammates are OK, so it was not theirs.'

Eva nodded. 'And the ending . . .' she said. 'They found what they needed?'

'Yes. They won.'

'Because they worked together,' Eva said. 'They dreamed in the same dream, right?'

'Exactly. They were compatible, able to understand each other in the Dreamscape,' the Professor explained.

'Who's compatible this time around?'

'We are working on that,' the Professor replied. 'We will announce the team by tomorrow.'

'I . . . I dreamed of Sam again last night.'

'Oh?'

'He was near an island,' Eva said. 'He was in the water—I saw him swimming towards a boat and then Tobias reached down to him to pull him aboard. Then everything flashed and blinded me. I couldn't see any more.'

'A blinding flash?' the Professor asked, concerned.

'Like fire swept over them, in a wave.'

'I'll have Jedi analyse the dream now, if that's OK?' the Professor said, and then his phone rang. 'Ah, the Dreamer Council about the competition details, I must take this.'

Eva nodded and stood. 'Thank you for showing me that dream.'

She left the office and walked towards her dorm, deep in thought. Try as she might, she couldn't shake the feeling that Sam needed her help.

SAM

Time seemed to slow as the seconds to hitting the ground stretched out before Sam's eyes. He threw his arms out onto the airbag and tucked his head down just as the ground sprang up to meet them.

Oh man!

They hit the park's grass nose-first, a colossal shudder running through the car and making Sam's teeth rattle. There was a moment when the car seemed to stand on its end, before slowing tipping over onto its roof.

Sam had to force his body to relax from its tensed position, the blood rushing to his head as he hung upside down.

I'm alive! I don't believe it!

Sam reached out and unbuckled the seatbelt, crashing to the upturned roof of the car and banging his head on the sunroof. Issey was groaning above in his seat, then the next moment he had landed next to Sam.

'Itai!' he groaned.

'Issey? Issey! Are you hurt?' Sam scrambled over as Issey's groaning intensified. Issey rolled over and gave

Sam a broad smile.

He isn't hurt, he's laughing!

'Woohoo!'

'Come on, you maniac, let's get out of here!' Sam sighed, kicking his door and rolling out onto the lawn. They emerged from the upside-down car and dusted themselves off.

'That was awesome!' Issey said, staggering away from the wreckage.

'Yeah,' Sam replied, his hands on his knees as he looked around and tried to regain his breath. 'That's, ah, one way to put it.'

Sam looked across to the pond—Stella's car was in there, way out in the centre, bubbling away as it sank.

'Yeah!' Issey jumped into the air at the sight. 'Take that, bad guy—or lady! Take that, bad lady!'

'We should keep moving,' Sam said, watching Stella's car disappear.

'Yes, yes, good,' Issey said. 'Keep moving. OK.'

'Issey, look at me,' Sam said. The Japanese Dreamer looked at him, and Sam could see that he was shaking with all the adrenalin. 'You need to calm down and get it together, you hear me? Because we won't always get away like that. Breathe, OK?'

Issey nodded.

'In a few minutes,' Sam said, 'there'll be cops here to arrest us. Or worse, Stella's guys will get to us first.'

'They're worse than cops, right?'

'Yes—far worse. Stealing a car and crashing it will be the least of our problems.'

'What would they do to us?' Issey asked.

'Nothing good,' Sam replied. 'Do you know anywhere safe we can get to from here?'

'Home.'

'Not your place, it'll be compromised, they'll know where you live. Someplace they won't be waiting for us.'

'I . . . ah . . .'

'Issey, it's alright. Calm down and think, this is *your* town. I'm sure you know someplace safe. We have to find someplace to hide, to rest, and so that you can dream.'

'Yes. OK, I know a place near here,' Issey replied, looking around the park. 'We can hide with him.'

'Nice. Come on, lead the way.' Sam took a last look at the top of Stella's car as it sank under the pond's surface.

Did she get out?

'Near here' turned out to be twenty minutes at a steady jog. Sam stopped outside the house with his hands on his knees and sucked in deep breaths.

'Too much American food, tomodachi,' Issey said.

Canadian . . . ah, whatever.

Issey rang the doorbell on an ancient-looking house in

a tree-lined street among other traditional Japanese three-storey houses that looked as if they could have come out of a picture book.

Sam looked around. It was night-time and no-one was on the streets.

He's managed to find a quiet neighbourhood in one of the world's busiest cities.

'My parents aren't like yours,' Sam said. 'As soon as they found out that I'd dreamed of Solaris, they called it in and had me picked up from school by a team of Agents with guns.'

'That sounds pretty amazing.'

'It might now, but at the time, I was pretty freaked out—nearly died, actually. The helicopter I was in crashed.'

Issey looked shocked.

'Tell you another time,' Sam said. 'So, who's this friend?' he asked, looking at the house.

'Oh, he's just the wisest guy in the universe.'

'The universe, you say?'

'Yes. And maybe the oldest, too. He's my grandfather.'

'Well, let's just hope he's home,' Sam said.

They waited a few minutes, then Issey pressed the bell for the fifth time.

'I think we should accept he's not in,' Sam said. 'Maybe he's so smart he saw this coming and decided to have no part in it.'

'He's in,' Issey said. 'He's always in.'

'Can you try calling him on a phone?'

'He has no phone,' Issey replied.

'No phones at all?'

'Nope.'

'You know, I always wanted to meet that guy,' Sam said.

'What guy?'

'The one person in the developed world with no phone.'

'Oh.' Issey looked confused.

They both jumped when the ancient door finally creaked opened as they stood there.

The oldest and smartest guy in the world stood before them. The oldest part certainly seemed right—with wisps of grey hair at his temples and creased lines across his weathered face.

'Ojiisama,' Issey said as he bowed deeply, Sam followed suit as Issey spoke to him in hushed Japanese for a moment. The old man's face lit up and he welcomed them in like they were the most cherished guests he had ever received.

'Kaga is much more than just my grandfather,' Issey explained. 'He coached me on my dreams and about fulfilling my destiny—he always thought that I would be one of the 13, even though my parents were unsure.'

'Cool—intense, though,' Sam said, and after removing their shoes they walked through to a tea room by an inner courtyard. A glorious blossoming tree stood majestically amid the carefully raked sandy ground. They sat on the floor at a low table, and Kaga poured them tea as Issey recounted what had happened.

'So, it is true,' Kaga said in lilting English. 'You are of the 13.'

'Yes,' Issey replied.

'And Sam-san, it is you that dreamed of Issey?'

'Yes.'

'Then you are the one who dreams of the others,' Kaga said.

'Yes, that's me,' Sam replied, and sipped his tea.

'I can see that you are very wise, Sam-san, wise far beyond your years,' Kaga said.

'Thanks. Many have said so.' Sam grinned.

'Humble, you are not.'

'I was just joking,' Sam said, embarrassed.

'That is good,' Kaga smiled. 'You will need to be wise, and a wise man has a sense of humour. You need to be complete to defeat the evil one.'

'Solaris?' Issey said.

Kaga nodded.

'You have met him?' Kaga asked Sam.

Sam nodded.

'And the fire . . .' Kaga said. 'Is it true—that he can make and send out fire?'

'Yes,' Sam said. 'I've seen it, up close. It's some sort of system built into his armoured suit.'

'And yet you survived,' Kaga said.

'I was lucky.'

Kaga shook his head. 'There is no luck, only destiny. You, Sam, must believe that you are destined to be there at the end, the final one. One of 13, yes, but also *the one.*'

'Yes,' Sam said. 'I believe it.'

Kaga smiled, and turned to Issey. 'And what number are you?'

'I—Sam?'

'Nine,' Sam answered for him. 'We have already found eight, Issey is the ninth to be found. But the numbers on the Gears count down so his Gear will be number five.'

'Then you are close to the end,' Kaga said, 'to your destiny.' He looked to Issey. 'And your dream, your part of the puzzle, you have seen it?'

'No,' Issey said, and he looked to the floor. 'Not yet.'

Kaga nodded. 'Yes. I see it in your sleepy eyes. Tonight the two of you will sleep here, where it is safe. Sleep, Issey. You will dream soon enough.'

ALEX

Alex landed flat on his back on the cab's bonnet. He gazed up at the sky spinning above him, listening to the howl of sirens and the blaring of horns.

'Ow,' Alex groaned quietly as he tried to move his aching body. Then reality came crashing back.

The bomb!

He looked at his wrist—

The bomb-wristband was gone.

As he struggled to get up, he spotted it on the ground in between the cars.

KLAP-BOOM!

Just then the wristband exploded, the force of it lifting the cab from the ground, throwing Alex back across the bonnet and rolling off the side and onto the road.

The car in front, a black limo, had its boot lid ripped off. As it flew high through the air, a fire erupted. The limo's petrol tank was punctured, fire slowly spreading across the road. People began screaming and running from the scene.

'Alex, here!' Shiva said. He got the motorbike upright again and kick-started, revving the engine.

Alex jumped on the back. 'Look, my wristband!' he said. 'It's gone!'

'I know!' Shiva replied, taking off, driving the bike through the wall of petrol flames. They were weaving through the traffic ahead and a block later the way cleared for Shiva to shift up gears, hitting fifty kilometres per hour, sixty, sixty-five . . .

'Somehow that crash severed it from my wrist!' Alex yelled into Shiva's ear. 'That was amazing!'

'I know!' Shiva replied over his shoulder.

'Then what's the rush?' Alex asked.

'This!' Shiva showed his left wrist.

We must be out of range of the apartment now. It's triggered the timer on his wristband.

It read:

4:04

4:03

4:02

Shiva threw down the bike in the side alley as he and Alex leaped off in one bound.

Shiva's wristband screen read:

1:13

1:12

1:11

'We made good time,' Alex said, looking around for any rogue Agents. 'You sure this is the place?'

'Pretty sure. Now we just have to hope Matrix's still here,' Shiva said while running, opening the fire door to the building and moving in fast. 'He could have popped out for sushi for all we know.'

'And we haven't got a minute to spare.'

'Dude, don't joke.'

They ran down the stairs to the heavy steel doors.

'Wait—what if there're goons in there?' Alex asked.

'There won't be, because we're the only ones who know this place is here. And they think we're trapped in the apartment, so they won't be expecting any trouble.'

'OK, let's do this,' Alex said.

'Shh, quiet as you can.' Shiva entered the combination and the doors clinked open.

Hacking really does come in handy.

They went through the doorway and down a steel staircase. The interior was a cavernous room, dark except for the far corner, where the glow of big computer screens showed the outline of a figure with his back to them.

Matrix.

Creeping silently, Shiva picked up a wrench and gave Alex a screwdriver.

What on earth will I do with a screwdriver?

0:49

Shiva covered the final few paces across the dusty concrete floor and swung the wrench.

There was a dull thud as Matrix slumped forwards, unconscious.

'The code!' Alex said. 'You need him for the code!'

Alex stole a glance at the timer:

0:44

'It's in his phone, that's how he set the devices,' Shiva said, grabbing Matrix's phone and scrolling through screens.

0:39

'Was it a numerical code?' Alex asked.

'No, an audible tone,' Shiva said. 'Aha!'

He pressed play on a file.

A tone sounded.

0:36

0:35

0:34

'There must be another!'

'I can't see it!' Shiva said, feverishly searching files, his hands shaking. It was the first time Alex had seen his friend truly panicked. 'I can't find it!'

0:31

0:30

0:29

SAM

'I don't think I can sleep,' Issey said.

Sam sighed. 'Probably not—not when you keep talking every other minute,' he muttered.

Issey was quiet for a moment. 'Can you sleep?' he asked.

Sam opened his eyes in the darkened room of Kaga's house. 'Why don't you just try being still and quiet for a while?' he said. 'Like, five minutes or so.'

'Hai . . . good idea.'

Issey's silence lasted a minute, before he said, 'You really think I will dream of the Gear?'

Sam turned over. They were in little roll-out beds on opposite sides of the room.

'Probably,' Sam said. 'With the other Dreamers, they had their Gear dream within one or two days of my dream of them, usually before, but hey, a pattern can always change. But I'm sure it'll be one or two days at the most.'

'Now is a day?'

'Not even yet, so try and relax, OK?'

'OK.'

'I mean it.'

'Yes.'

Sam lay in silence, Issey too. Nearly an hour had passed by the time Sam heard the newest Dreamer sleeping. At first, Issey was silent, then he started sleep-talking, which kept Sam awake. Issey spoke in Japanese, with lots of laughter, and then came some English.

'Look out, Solaris—I am Samurai warrior! I am Ronin, now I kick your butt, hahaha!'

After that the snoring resumed.

Great. No sleep for me tonight.

Sam looked up out of the little window above his bed, where clouds were scattered in the night, lit from underneath by the city lights.

Tobias is out there somewhere, leading the chase away from us. He and the Guardians are out there fighting and running and chasing, and—

Sam's mind went blank. All his concentration went to his senses—to listening.

He heard it again. A creaking sound from downstairs.

The front door?

Sam knew that he'd seen Kaga go to bed when they did, in the room down the hall at the top of the stairs.

So unless he silently walked down the stairs and decided to go for a midnight stroll, it's not likely to be him.

And there was no-one else in the house.

Sam slipped out of bed and moved silently to their door. As he moved, he changed his Stealth Suit to black, melting into the shadows and staying there.

He peered down the hallway, lit by the grey light coming in through the glass wall that bordered the courtyard.

He saw no movement.

But he heard it. A wary footfall downstairs—someone trying to move around stealthily in an unfamiliar space.

Someone's definitely in the house.

Movement caught his eye—down the hall, Kaga opened his door. He was pulling on a silver metal suit with a helmet and mask, like firefighters used to walk into fires. He motioned with his hands for Sam to get Issey and to escape another way.

Through the window?

Sam hesitated a moment but then nodded. The old man finished off his suit, pulling on silver gloves, and picking up a fire extinguisher in one hand and a long wooden pole in the other before making for the stairs.

It was then that Sam realised Kaga knew who was downstairs. He choked on the realisation.

Solaris.

How Kaga had known Solaris would one day show up here, and how and why he prepared for this moment, Sam would never know. But he knew that the old man was sacrificing himself so that the two Dreamers could escape.

It will not be for nothing.

Sam crept back into their room and shook Issey awake. 'We have to get out of here,' he whispered, dragging Issey out of bed and throwing his clothes to him.

'What?' Issey was dazed, trying to comprehend what Sam was saying.

'Shh, we have to leave, now!'

'But Grandfather—' Issey protested.

'He is staying here. Hurry,' Sam urged. He pulled Issey to the window and opened it. Outside was the sloping roof, high above the ground.

'Why can't we just—'

The room lit up in bright orange as fire roared up the staircase and spilled down the hall.

Sam and Issey both looked back through the open bedroom doorway to see Kaga at the top of the stairs, fire engulfing him. Slowly, the old man descended, one deliberate step at a time, an occasional blast of foam from the fire extinguisher gushing out before him.

The suit is fireproof!

Kaga twirled the wooden staff in his other hand—a samurai, walking into battle.

'OK,' Issey said, and then rushed out the window.

Sam was frozen on the spot for a moment, the image of a man walking into the fire forever burned into his mind. He shook it off, and followed Issey out onto the roof.

Sam slipped almost immediately.

Oh man . . . come on, Sam, concentrate.

Fire lit up the house again. Sam clung tight to a handhold and kept up with Issey. A fall to the cobbled street below would be bone-breaking, and the ledge that they had to scale across to get to the next house's roof was no more than two centimetres wide.

Sam followed Issey's movements, shuffling sideways, clinging to the wall, and as they neared the edge of Kaga's house, the roof descended to the point where they could now hold onto the eaves overhead.

'We have to use the roof!' Sam called. Issey understood, letting his feet dangle free and hanging on just with his hands. He shimmied along the last couple of metres to the edge of the roof that slightly overhung its neighbour. 'Now swing over!' Sam urged.

Issey started to rock his legs back and forth, building up momentum, then letting go as his feet dangled over the next roof. He landed with a thud, grabbing onto the roof tiles so as not to slip. He turned onto his back and motioned Sam over.

Sam made the same movements, kicking off the wall with his feet and using his hands over his head to carry his weight along the edge of the eaves. He was almost at the far edge of the roof when the window below him shattered and fire swept out with immense heat.

He lifted his feet as another jet shot out. The heat was so close, Sam could feel it searing into the cold night air.

A whooshing noise rippled out and white foam erupted from the window, followed by noises of a struggle. Through the window, Sam could see Solaris and Kaga engaged in a hand-to-hand fight. The short man in his shiny silver suit was tackling the tall black-clad figure. Solaris was blocking Kaga's blows with his forearms and then kicking and punching in retaliation.

'Sam, jump!'

Sam looked across to Issey. He swung his legs back and forth in a pendulum motion, mimicking what he had been taught more than a decade before by his parents on the swing at their local park as a young boy. When the angle seemed right, he let go, swinging through the air legs-first, his feet hitting the edge of the roof tiles—

The tiles slipped out from under his feet, clattering to the ground more than ten metres below.

Oh no!

There was an odd moment when Sam felt he was done for, in a kind of freefall as his feet moved on a never-ending treadmill of tiles that disappeared from under him, and that he was slowly tilting back, destined to fall backwards—

'Argh!' Sam shifted his weight forward.

'Here!' Issey said as he grabbed onto Sam's wrist, but he pulled Issey down too.

'Hang onto something!' Sam cried out as they began sliding down the roof, the ceramic tiles smashing in the street below as fire continued to spill from next door.

Issey turned and grabbed onto the roof, pulling Sam forward enough so that together they could scramble up to the ridge where they settled and looked back at Kaga's house.

'We have to go back and help Grandfather!' Issey said.

'No,' Sam replied, watching as bursts of flames erupted from the top-floor windows. 'He's fighting so that you can escape. We have to get out of here.'

'I can't leave him in there.'

'You can, and you have to,' Sam said, his voice definite, and Issey looked him in the eyes. 'You have to fulfil your destiny, as Kaga said. If we wait any longer here, it will be too late—for you, for me, for everyone.'

Issey wavered for a moment, looking back at the house, then turned and started moving away, over the ridge and to the next house, fast, and Sam followed. In just two minutes they'd jumped from roof to roof to get to the end of the block, where they took a rainwater pipe down to the ground like it was a fireman's pole.

The intersection here was as quiet as the rest of the neighbourhood, but there was the far-off sound of fire-engines.

'Issey, we have to keep moving,' Sam said, seeing that Issey was looking down the street to the red-orange glow. 'Issey?'

'Yes. Yes.' He looked at Sam with a new determination. 'Sam, I had my dream.'

'Of the Gear?'

'Yes.'

'You know where it is?'

'I think so. I need to think about it—to sit and think.'

'We'll find someplace quiet and safe, and we'll sort out our next step.'

Issey nodded, looking up and down the street. 'He's going to pay,' he said. 'This Solaris guy, he's going to pay.'

EVA

Eva sat in a small classroom with the last 13—Gabriella, Xavier, Zara, Rapha, Maria, Cody and Arianna.

'Usually the Dreamer Doors competition has teams of three students from each of the four Academies, competing in the previous champion's dream to find a prize,' Lora said. 'This year will be different—your team, under the guise of the competition, will use the constructed Dreamscape to try to find the Gears that have fallen into the wrong hands.'

'How do we do that?' Xavier asked.

'The Dreamscape that is created will feel like ordinary, waking life, and you will all share in it. The very nature of the constructed dream will assist you in your search for the Gears. Having those connected minds all together in there will magnify your dreamwaves and hopefully draw you to the Gears in a way you would struggle to do in real life.'

'Sounds good!' Rapha said.

'So it'll feel like we're in another reality?' Eva said.

'Yes. You'll be aware it's a dream, but it will feel completely real,' Lora said, 'like the lucid dreams that you have been having in my classes. There is one important extra element though.'

Lora brought up a digital image onto the screen at the front of the classroom.

'These doors are scattered throughout the construct world,' she explained, pointing to the images of a white door and a black door at different locations. 'The white doors will take you where you want to go.'

'Whoa, hang on . . .' Xavier said. *'Anywhere?'*

'Almost, although you must have your destination clear in your mind. But for argument's sake, if you need to get from this door to say, a door nearest the Opera House in Sydney, then you picture it in your mind as you open the door and go through.'

'And if we *don't* have a clear mental picture?' Eva said. 'Or if we just run through without an idea?'

'Then you will end up at any one of the thousands of doors around the world,' Lora said. 'And the disorientation may cause you to go back through the door, only to find yourself at another location, and so on. So it's of the utmost importance to be focused and calm when using the white doors.'

'What about the black doors?' Gabriella asked.

Lora nodded and zoomed in on the picture of the black door. 'They number less, about five thousand all up, scattered around the world,' she said. 'Again, you must concentrate, but they do one of two things.'

Eva sat on the edge of her chair, waiting.

'First, they can bring you back to your waking life, and you will be out of the competition. For instance, if you manage to find the location of a Gear, you can use a black door to immediately come out of the construct. And if, for whatever reason, you feel you can go no further in the game, you can come back, there is no harm in that.'

'How long does each tournament last?'

'Until the Dreamer prize is found and brought back through a black door,' Lora explained, showing a picture of some past prizes—a compass, a large, ornate book and a miniature die-cast car.

'Funny prizes,' Zara said.

'I don't understand the toy car,' Maria said.

'The prize is to win the game—the actual object is not the aim. It could be anything, and it'll be something different this year,' Lora explained. 'The trick is that with each of the three rounds, the number of white doors decreases by half. The record in over a hundred years of the Dreamer Doors is five days in the construct.'

'Wow,' Maria said.

'What is the other thing the black doors do?' Gabriella asked.

'Good question,' Lora said. 'If you choose to go through a black door to combat your worst nightmare, you go back through the door to the construct, where you will find the number of white doors has grown a hundred times over.

It's also how you can summon your back-up partner, who will then remain with you and your team until the next black door.'

'So it's kinda like a hack,' Xavier said. 'Excellent.'

'No,' Eva said. 'Not a hack. It's a gamble. If you take the chance to face your nightmare, you might end up getting kicked out of the game if you fail. Right, Lora?'

'That's correct,' Lora said.

'So if you die in the game, if the nightmare beats you, you're out?' Zara asked.

'You wake up and the team is down to two players, and then perhaps to one.'

'For the rest of the tournament?' Cody asked, tentatively joining in the conversation.

'Yes,' Lora said. 'Once you're dead in the construct, your part in the Dreamer Doors is over.'

'Then we agree not to take unnecessary risks,' Eva said to her teammates. 'OK?'

They all nodded in agreement.

'So,' Lora said. 'Next up, some geography lessons—and make no mistake, the Eastern Academy is renowned for their speedy use of the white doors, so you'd all better brush up on your major cities, towns and landmarks.'

'Huh,' Gabriella said. 'Time for more homework . . .'

Eva scrolled through the images of landmarks on her laptop and mentally mapped them to the cities they were in and or near to. She felt confident that if chosen to compete in the competition, she would use the white doors well. The others were spread out around the room, each face illuminated by a screen and creased with concentration.

'OK,' Lora said, re-entering the room. 'The team has been decided. Xavier, your Gear fell into the hands of Solaris in Germany—'

'Yep, thanks for reminding me,' he interrupted. 'Not my finest hour.'

'—so you will be one of our three to compete,' Lora finished.

'Yes!' Xavier stood and pumped his fists into the air. 'Here I come, Dreamer Doors!'

'And Zara, your Gear is also with Solaris, as is the Bakhu box itself,' Lora said, 'so you will be our second team member.'

'Oui, d'accord. I understand,' Zara said, straightening up in her chair.

'Finally, as the two of you are searching out your Gears, the last team member will need to be going after the prize itself, to make sure the construct stays open long enough for you to find your Gears,' Lora said. 'Eva, that will be you.'

Eva felt her face flush red. 'Sure, good.'

Xavier gave her a friendly nudge with his shoulder. 'In it together, Dream Girl,' he smiled.

'The remainder of you will be the support team,' Lora said, 'and may be called upon as back-up as each player can call on one assistant to enter and help out during each phase, though for a limited period only.'

'This sounds complicated,' Arianna said.

'It will become clearer,' Lora replied, 'I promise. But you should understand that although this is a game, it's not child's play. In terms of difficulty and skill, think of it like the Olympics.'

'It's our Olympics of dreams . . .' Xavier said.

'We still have a little time to continue to coach you before the first round begins in a few days,' Lora said. 'We must make the most of it so you are *all* as ready as you can be.'

SAM

'**S**omeplace quiet' turned out to be a tiny cafe. Even in the middle of the night, it was filled with about fifty people crammed onto stools or standing in a space that would be a tight squeeze for twenty. Sam texted their location to Tobias and he got a message back almost instantly.

Stay put. Be there in 10.

'What do you remember from your dream?' Sam asked, seated at the end of a bar next to Issey, the two of them trying to drink iced tea while they caught their breath after their frantic escape.

'It is as if I saw a vision of the past,' Issey said, sipping his tea. 'The Gear? I think it was part of something for navigating. There was a trading ship, tall with sails, old-fashioned. It docked at an island here in Japan. The whole scene was from another time, hundreds of years ago. Then, the device was left behind, and then . . . then . . .'

Sam let Issey take the time to recall the dream, and he couldn't help but think of the ship he'd seen with Maria.

How many Gears were turned into other devices? And what

will we do if it turns out that one is lost on a ship wreck? Sift through five hundred years of silt on the ocean floor?

'Like any dream,' Sam said, 'the further you are from it, the fewer details you can remember. But it will return.'

'Return?'

'Tobias will meet us here, and we'll go someplace safe, where we can hook you up to a dream-reading machine.'

'OK—my parents have one,' Issey said, texting on his own phone. 'They just pinged me, they're with Tobias and nearly here now.'

Issey stared into his drink.

'You're thinking about Kaga,' Sam said.

'Yes,' Issey admitted. 'I am. I feel so guilty that we left him, alone, against that—that fire-breathing thing.'

'Kaga knew what he was doing,' Sam said. 'He was prepared to face Solaris, you know that. It's like he knew it was his destiny, his part in this.'

Issey was silent.

'You know I'm right, right?' Sam repeated. 'I just met him, but it was obvious he was smart, prepared and he was ready. Maybe he even kicked Solaris' butt back there, saved us all a big headache. He'll be knighted, get medals, probably have his face put on postage stamps for the work he did. Or a whole series of manga books celebrating his achievements—computer games, maybe.'

Issey allowed himself a small smile.

'Look, this is . . .' Sam trailed off.

What else can I say?

'You have to live out your dream now,' Sam said, 'then you have to keep going so that when the time comes, when we eventually get to the Dream Gate, we can all do what has to be done.'

'I know that this is not like what I usually do—it's not a game.'

Sam made a show of being surprised. 'I thought your games were more than that. I thought it was a sport, a profession.'

'Yes,' Issey said, breaking into a grin. 'Yes, OK, I admit it. I have been playing around with *games* all these years. You know, a few hours ago, gaming was my whole world. I thought what I did was making people happy. I thought it was the most important thing.'

Sam nodded, then signalled for another round of tea.

'I think,' Issey said, 'that my gaming was like a quick moment of happiness. What we are doing now, with this dreaming, finding this Gear and unlocking the mysteries of so long ago, is permanent. It is literally . . . life and death, yes?'

'Sure is,' Sam said. 'And if we don't succeed? Then someone else will.' He stared outside into the night. Heavy rain was falling, the coloured neon lights of the laneway of bars and eateries melding into a futuristic multi-coloured haze. 'I see Tobias,' he said, getting up to make the introductions as Tobias came in.

Tobias looked relieved to see them unharmed. He was drenched from the deluge outside. 'Sorry it took me so long,' he said, changing his Stealth Suit to a lighter material in the warm bar, leaving a rather large puddle on the floor from the rain.

'Where are my parents?' Issey asked.

'They dropped me around the corner from here, they're headed to a safe house.'

'Oh,' Issey said.

'We had to be sure we weren't being followed,' Tobias said. 'I walked round ten blocks to get here, and they're going to drive through the backstreets. Stella has her Agents everywhere looking for us.'

'So we must make our steps very carefully,' Issey said.

'That's right,' Tobias said. 'Stay off phones unless they're secure. Be careful not to be caught on security cameras, that kind of thing.'

'Really?' Issey said.

'Yes,' Sam replied. 'Stella has a computer genius working for her, and he's able to track us by hacking into cameras all over the world and finding our faces through facial recognition software.'

'I'll take that,' Tobias said, taking Issey's phone and dropping it into a glass of iced tea as Issey's jaw dropped. 'Even the camera here in this cafe, in the corner behind you? If it's linked to a security system with links to the internet, then Matrix will find a way to access it.'

'Oh,' Sam said, feeling foolish for not thinking of that.

'Or you could be identified in the background of someone's photo if they post it online,' Tobias said. 'Matrix's programs will match your face and then work out the time of the photo and location, then they'll pull down data from every camera in the area to map your movements, then—*bam!*'

Tobias clapped his hands together.

'So we'd better leave,' Sam said, standing, trying to shield his face from the camera but knowing it'd be too late anyway.

'Stick close,' Tobias replied, pushing the door open.

'Where is this safe house?' Issey asked.

'Your parents said to meet where you went for your thirteenth birthday,' Tobias replied, as they slipped out onto the street.

Issey looked puzzled and Sam worried that perhaps the message was too vague.

'Aha!' Issey said, smiling triumphantly in the rain. 'Of course!'

'You know where to go?' Sam said, adding a hood to his Stealth Suit.

'Oh, yes,' Issey replied. 'That and more! While I was busy thinking about something else, my mind has remembered where the next Gear is.'

ALEX

0:17
Matrix made a sound, stirring awake—the blow to the back of the head had obviously not rendered him entirely unconscious.

Alex grabbed him around the collar, shaking him. 'The code!' he yelled. 'What is it?'

'Never.'

0:14

Shiva put the wristband and digital read-out right in front of Matrix's eyes, which opened wide when he realised what was about to happen.

0:13

Shiva passed Matrix the phone.

0:12

Matrix fumbled the phone, his hands shaking as he tried to punch in a code.

0:08

'Come on!' Alex gasped. He saw Shiva starting to pull away from them, to shield them from the blast.

No!

Matrix's sweat dripped onto the handset as he keyed in a code.

0:05

The phone made a series of loud beeps and then—

0:02.

The countdown stopped.

There was a heavy moment of silence. Matrix collapsed on the floor in shock, Shiva simply stood stock-still, looking at the wristband. Then Alex began whooping.

'That was *unbelievable!*' he shouted out. 'That was out of sight crazy! Did you see *that?*'

'See it—I was there!' Shiva replied, now falling to the ground in a heap, putting his head between his legs. He sat back up suddenly, reaching for pliers on a nearby table. He used them to remove the wristband, breaking the two straps at the clasp and both wires with it. Then he slumped down once more.

'It—it stopped at two seconds!' Alex was dancing around from foot to foot.

'I know, nail-biting stuff, eh?' Shiva tried to laugh through his shock.

'Hey, you! Don't you even think about it!' Alex said to Matrix, hefting the big wrench above his head.

Matrix raised his hands in surrender. 'Don't hurt me,' he whined.

'Hold on, there's something I've always wanted to do,' Shiva said, getting up to run gaffer tape around Matrix's arms and around the back of the office chair, spinning him around until it was about fifteen layers thick.

'You pathetic idiots,' Matrix spat out. 'You don't even understand what you're up against!'

'Really, you always wanted to tape up your boss?' Alex said, ignoring Matrix and inspecting his friend's handiwork. 'That's just weird.'

'Figure of speech,' Shiva replied. 'But I have always wanted to whack him over the head with a wrench ever since I knew he was a traitor.'

Matrix fell silent.

Shiva went to the computers, checking over the coding Matrix had been running.

'No way . . .' he said.

'What was he up to?' Alex asked.

'He's . . . he's rewired Tesla's Dream Coils not to see into the Dreamscape, but to work in reverse.'

'Huh?'

'Look here,' Shiva said, scrolling through dozens of pages of code. 'This is almost the opposite of what I was doing, which was what the machines were designed to do.'

'To look into dreams?' Alex added.

'Right. Well, somehow they've managed to capture certain dreams and send them back out into the Dream-scape,' Shiva said. 'I'd heard rumours for years that this sort of thing was in development. I mean, we can record dreams, even on large scales, but to transmit a dream back into the Dreamscape? I mean, that's . . .'

'Science fiction,' Alex concluded.

'You never *were* that smart,' Matrix sneered.

Shiva ignored him.

'Why would Stella want to do this?' Alex asked.

'I don't know . . . could be a number of reasons.'

'Like?'

'Sending nightmares out into the world,' Shiva suggested.

'You think so *small*,' Matrix said. '*Anyone* could do that, and even with this tech, Tesla could have done it a century ago.'

'So it's about locating the Dreamers,' Shiva said, 'the rest of the last 13.' He stopped. 'No, it's something more than that . . . something so big that you would need to tap into the entire Dreamscape. The Academy? No, it has to be bigger, global . . .'

'I know what they're trying to do,' Alex said, breaking into a smile of realisation. 'You're right, it *is* global.'

Matrix's face looked ashen as it became obvious that Alex had figured it out.

I knew all that reading up about the Academy and the Dreamer world was going to come in handy.

Alex looked from Matrix to Shiva and said, 'They're going to hijack the Dreamer Doors.'

SAM

Tobias packed away the dream recorder, and Sam was puzzled.

'It was so dark,' Sam said, 'are you sure you know the location?'

'Yes,' Issey said, looking to his parents, who nodded. They and Tobias were all seated at the 'safe house'—the ticket booth of an amusement park, closed for the night.

Sam had taken an instant liking to Issey's parents, Haruto and Megumi. They were both elegantly dressed in suits—Haruto tall and strong with square glasses and a serious smile, Megumi much shorter, with long flowing hair and a handshake Sam could trust.

Agents or not, they seem like good people.

'You think it's on an island?' Tobias was saying.

'We went there once, for a tour, with some school friends, remember, father?'

'I do,' Haruto replied. 'That was a good trip.'

'Good, but you two were scared,' Megumi added.

'It's scary?' Sam said.

'We camped for the night on the island,' Issey explained to Sam and Tobias. 'It was like a haunted tour, and going there we were all laughing and joking about who would have nightmares.'

'But then, through the night, we heard the sounds,' Haruto said.

'Sounds?' Sam said, remembering the guttural growls that he'd heard in his own dream of Issey.

'They were not natural,' Issey said. 'No animal I've ever heard.'

Issey's mother laughed. 'My boys, scared of things that come out at night.'

'You were not there, my dear,' her husband said.

'There are reasons why the island was deserted,' Issey said. 'We'd heard stories—and then we heard the actual sounds.'

'Surely they wouldn't let tourists go there to camp if there was some kind of real danger?' Tobias said.

'The noises came from underground,' Issey's father said, 'from the tunnels and rooms that are carved throughout the rock and down under the sea.'

'And you're sure *that's* where your dream led you?' Sam asked.

'I'm sure of it,' Issey said. 'I will never forget that place. The dream felt like it was another time, but the island was the place.'

'OK,' Sam said, getting up. 'We've no time to waste,

because the longer we wait around, the more chance Stella or Solaris has of catching up with us.'

'Agreed,' Tobias said. 'Although we'll need to stock up on some supplies.'

'No need,' Haruto said, and he led them over to his car. He opened the boot and removed a large rucksack. In it were several torches, helmets, climbing gear, backpacks, rations, GPS units and more.

'It's my dad's emergency survival pack,' Issey explained, pride in his voice. 'Always ready for the next tsunami, nuclear meltdown or zombie apocalypse.'

'And whatever we might face,' Sam said. 'OK, get us to this island.'

'On the way,' Issey's father said, 'perhaps I can use your phone, Tobias? I would very much like to try to reach Kaga. We are very worried about him.'

'Of course,' Tobias said, handing over his phone.

Sam walked on with the others, fearful that Haruto would not hear good news.

Sam finished throwing up as the island came into sight.

'Some hero, hey?' he said to Issey, who was hanging onto him as he stood at the rail of the boat, heaving up and down and side to side in the stormy black sea.

'I used to get seasick too,' Issey said, 'but I've been

fishing with my dad so long now that I'm used to it. This is a bad night and the storm doesn't help, if that makes you feel better?'

Sam nodded, still feeling too ill to leave the side of the boat. The boat taking them to the island was a small fishing vessel, big enough to hold maybe ten people, with a small covered pilot house and an area below deck with bunk beds. Haruto was steering, while Megumi and Tobias were holding on and looking quite pale themselves as the boat hit wave after wave and was battered by the strong squalls.

'How do we get up *there*?' Sam said loudly into Issey's ear, pointing to the top of the cliffs ahead of them, where he could just make out the shapes of buildings.

'The other side,' Issey yelled back. 'There's a small jetty, and a cage elevator up the side.'

Sam swallowed against more rising bile. The island looked like it was built to withstand all manner of attacks. The sheer rock walls rose twenty metres above the sea, the constructed stone and concrete walls another twenty or thirty metres above that. There were very few openings in the rocks that Sam could see, but there was not much light to see by.

At least my feet will be on solid ground.

Lightning lit the sky and the clouds opened up with a heavy deluge of rain, the likes of which Sam had never felt.

'Any news on Kaga yet?' Sam shouted in Issey's ear.

'No,' he replied, looking out to sea. 'The fire department is still putting out the fire.'

'He might be OK, you know.'

Issey nodded.

Sam looked up at the island as they neared and started to sail around to the other side, the swell of the waves now hitting against their wooden-hulled boat broadside, the rocking side-to-side so intense that he had to hold on with both hands to avoid behind thrown overboard.

'This place is known as Obakeshima,' Issey yelled over the wind, the island no longer sheltering them from its full force. 'It once had government staff working here, but then it became completely deserted, practically overnight.'

'Why?'

'Lots of stories, but no-one seems to know for sure.'

'Very mysterious. It looks like a fortress!' Sam yelled, the boat turning again, this time the waves breaking behind it, pushing against the stern and sweeping them fast towards the tiny concrete jetty, almost indistinguishable against the wild seas and dark craggy rock and concrete walls.

Time to find out what's really on this island.

They neared the island's jetty and Issey's father threw the boat's engine into full reverse, but it was too late. In the fierce weather that was rapidly getting worse, a wave surged them towards the pier.

Sam moved away from the side of the boat that was heading in—

Way too fast!

'Hold on!' Tobias yelled.

The boat slammed against massive truck tyres tied against the pier, sending the wooden craft bouncing back out to sea, the reversing engine countering the effect of the waves as Issey's father navigated back to shore.

'Okaasan!' Issey called out, and Sam watched as his friend rushed to help his mother who was on the floor of the boat, holding onto her arm.

'It's broken,' Tobias said to Haruto after administering first aid. 'Can we tie the boat to the pier and get onto more stable ground?'

'It'll be smashed into toothpicks by the waves against that pier, tyres or no tyres,' he answered. 'I can drop you off and head out to wait in calmer water on the other side of the island, and pick you up later.'

Tobias looked from Issey's mother to the jetty and then to Sam. 'OK,' he said. 'Sam, you and Issey make your way up to the complex. I'll take Megumi around to the sheltered side of the island and take care of her arm. Then we'll come back around and I'll follow you up in the elevator.'

'Shouldn't we stick together?' Sam said.

'We can send the elevator back down once we're up there,' Issey said. 'It only takes ten minutes to go down and come back up.'

Only?

'Take us in again, Haruto,' Tobias said. He took over cradling Megumi from Issey, who readied himself by the bow with Sam.

'Be quick as you can!' Sam shouted, then he jumped ashore as the boat neared, sprinting along the concrete pier, Issey close behind. They turned and waved off the boat, which was already heading out of the tiny harbour.

'Follow me!' Issey said and led the way forwards, the reflective patches on his backpack flashing under the beam of Sam's torch.

Sam almost ran into a small sign as they skidded to the base of the cliff. He shone the torch onto it.

Issey stopped beside him. 'Here we are,' he said.

'What's with the graffiti?' Sam asked.

'That's what it means in English,' Issey replied.

Ghost Island? Are you kidding me?

Sam turned back to where the pier ended in a vertical concrete slab, almost as though it came from the sea and up the wall. There was a metal track with notched teeth set into it, where the elevator would slowly make its journey.

But there was no elevator.

'You said your father knew the island's superintendent.'

'He does,' Issey yelled, shining his flashlight up, but its beam was lost in the rain before it could find the bottom of the elevator.

'I thought he organised for the elevator to be down here and the generator on?' Sam said, holding onto a rail bolted into the concrete to stop himself from being blown off the pier in the hurricane winds.

'He *did!*'

'Then where's the elevator?'

Issey cast his light in front of them and found a call button set into the wall and pulled the large lever to the down position. Large, well-greased chains started to move alongside the teethed track.

'It's coming down!' Issey said.

Sam didn't like it. Didn't like all of this—the weather, the accident with Issey's mum that changed their plans and he certainly didn't like that the elevator was not where it was meant to be.

The weather and the accident that followed could not have been avoided.

But this could have. Either their friend forgot, or something came up.

'Maybe it was the weather!' Issey said, close enough into Sam's ear to be heard over the crashing sound of the waves breaking against concrete and stone. 'Maybe he had to go back up to check on something!'

'Yeah,' Sam replied. 'Maybe.'

They didn't have to wait long. Five minutes, to be exact. At the four-minute mark they could make out the bottom of the elevator as it slowly clinked its way down. About the size of a phone box, it had a solid steel bottom panel, while the sides and door were like a chain-link fence.

When it got to the ground and set down, the electric motor stopped and the chain was silent in the wind.

Neither Issey nor Sam was in a rush to open the door because on the floor of the elevator was a helmet. A white safety helmet, like you'd see on a construction site.

And it was splattered with blood.

At the top, the elevator stopped, the metallic clink-clink-clink of the chains running through the huge toothed wheel ended with a dull thud.

Sam cringed as he looked around, expecting a grizzly find—perhaps a body . . . that of the island's superintendent.

Instead, by the tight, bright beams of their flashlights against the dark, they found nothing but an open, rainswept courtyard, surrounded by concrete buildings that towered over them and shut out much of the wind.

Empty of life and devoid of a body.

Everything was quiet and still but for the squalls of rain and wind that lashed against the buildings.

'Maybe he just banged his head?' Sam said to Issey. 'That'd explain the helmet. He might have slipped in this weather.'

Issey nodded, then pointed over to a set of double doors set into a squat concrete building. They were big, heavy steel doors and one was ajar.

Sam and Issey ran across the courtyard towards it.

Issey slipped over on the wet ground, his flashlight

clattering across the concrete and rolling to a stop around a dark corner.

Sam helped his new friend to his feet, and together they made their way, slower this time, across the wet ground to retrieve the flashlight. As they neared, they could see its light shining down a tight alleyway between two tall buildings—

'Stop!' Sam whispered into Issey's ear, grabbing onto his arm. They stood dead still.

'What is it?' Issey asked, spooked.

'There . . .' Sam shone his torch in front, into a corner where a shoe was visible.

'It's just an old shoe,' Issey said. He went forward a few paces and picked up his flashlight.

The shoe twitched.

What the . . ?

Issey was frozen, stunned like a deer in the headlights.

Sam could see from his position that the shoe was attached to a leg. And that leg, to a body. It was moving, slowly. It was being *dragged* into the alley.

Dragged by . . .

'What is *that*?' Sam gasped. Their lights picked out a large, dark shape, hunched over the body. It was indistinguishable in the rain and from that distance. Then their flashlights picked out two shining spots.

A pair of eyes.

Huge, green-yellow and staring right back at them.

'*Run!*' Issey yelled, already passing Sam.

'I'm running!' Sam yelled, skidding on the ground as they threw themselves towards the double doors, squeezing inside and slamming the doors shut behind them—

BOOM!

The doors shook from a huge impact.

BOOM!

They backed away.

The air smelled of wet dog and bad breath.

Sam and Issey remained silent and still, and after a moment all seemed quiet. Sam pulled off his backpack, retrieving the dart pistol.

Whatever it was, it's gone for now. But if it's smart, it might be looking for another way in here.

The doors were hinged to open outwards, so ramming them from outside would not immediately threaten them. Examining the doors, Sam could see the steel was thick, perhaps built during the last war to be sturdy enough to withstand explosions.

'What is that out there?' Sam asked. 'I thought you were joking about hearing noises on the island.'

'There was nothing like *that* here before—when I came. I can't believe it. It was the beast you told me about from your nightmare! Here, in real life . . .' Issey said, and he started to hyper-ventilate.

'Calm down, Issey, it'll be OK, yeah?' Sam said, shining his light around the corridors that peeled off left and right, long and dark. But at least they appeared to be alone.

We have to find the Gear and get off this island as quickly as we can.

'It . . . it was eating someone—'

'Issey, I need you to get it together,' Sam said. 'Please, can you? You have to try. You need to focus right now, OK? Look at me. Focus, calm down. That's it . . .'

Issey took a deep breath and nodded, then started to choke.

'Shh, it's OK,' Sam said, his arm around Issey's shoulders.

BANG!

'It's going to get in here!' Issey cried.

'Those doors are strong,' Sam said. 'Besides, it's no monster or nightmare beast. I think it was a dog.'

There are no such things as monsters. The monsters we have to worry about are human.

'A dog?'

'OK, a *big* dog. But it had fur, it had a coat like a dog. And the eyes—and the smell.'

'A *dog*—eating a man?' Issey sounded unconvinced.

'Maybe it was trying to help him,' Sam said. 'To try and wake him up.'

Is he buying this?

'And what does it want with *us?*'

'Maybe it's the island guard dog and it sees us as

intruders,' Sam said. 'If he's just doing his job, we have to do ours. We have to find that Gear.'

Issey wasn't hearing Sam, and if he was he certainly wasn't comprehending anything that he was saying.

'That wasn't the superintendent,' Sam said.

'It wasn't?' Issey said. 'How do you know?'

'Because that person was in a uniform,' Sam said. 'The uniform of Stella's Agents. Which means that they're here, already, they're ahead of us.'

'But . . . how?'

'Honestly, I don't know right now. I'm sure we could figure it out,' Sam said, 'but this is not the time to do that. Right now your mum is down there in a boat, injured.' As Sam spoke, his tone was full of reason. 'We have to work together, and fast, before anyone else gets hurt, OK?'

'OK.'

'Good. Now, where's the Gear?' Sam said, his voice now trying to soothe and convince Issey to push on. 'Where is it? Where do we need to go?'

'I . . .' Issey said, looking around, his expression blank. He looked down to the floor when he said to Sam in a quiet voice. 'I know it is on the island. I saw it in a room, as part of something else, but I'm sorry, Sam—I'm not sure where to start looking.'

ALEX

'We all know that she's somehow been tapping into dreams, right?' Alex said into his phone. 'Stella, I mean. And we know now what she's attempting to do next.'

'And what is that?' Lora asked, her voice crackling with static interference. Alex was making the call from just outside the heavy doors of Matrix's secret lair, the first place he could find to get at least passable phone reception.

'It's about the Dreamer Doors—she's going to try to take it over,' Alex explained.

'Alex? Alex, you're breaking up,' Lora replied. 'Can . . . you get to . . . video . . ?'

'Sorry?'

'Can you make a video call?' Lora repeated, this time coming through clear enough for Alex to make out her voice.

'Yes, I think so.'

'I'll text you . . . details,' Lora said, hanging up.

Alex went back inside. They'd gagged Matrix so that he wouldn't disturb them, and then gaffer-taped his office chair to a column. The three towering Tesla Coils hummed with the energy coursing through them. Every now and then a thin blue line of electricity would crackle and spark between them. He could only imagine the scene in here when they were turned from standby to full operating power.

'How'd your phone call go?' Shiva asked.

'Terrible reception,' Alex said.

'It's the Coils, they're only running at less than five per cent, but it's enough to disrupt electronic signals and microwaves within a half-block radius.'

'Geez, no wonder Tesla never really got this thing fully operational,' Alex said, passing over his phone with the details of the video-call address. 'Can you link us up to the Academy via video?'

'Yep, give me a sec,' Shiva said, setting up the program on Matrix's laptop.

'Where'd they link into the power grid?' Alex asked, seeing the massive power cables snaking out of the room and down into the city works system. 'City Hall, like we did?'

'Nope, that power wasn't enough,' Shiva replied.

'They needed *more?*'

'They needed more, *and* a supply that was more resilient to the surges as each of the old Coils kicked in.'

'So where'd they find that kind of power down here?' Alex asked.

'The New York Stock Exchange,' Shiva said.

'Oh, man.'

'OK, here, video-calling them now,' Shiva said. It took a few seconds and then the call was answered.

Lora's face came up on the screen. Despite the electronic shielding case on the computer, the image on the screen was still like a slightly out of tune TV.

'OK, we see you,' Lora said.

'And we're reading you,' Shiva replied.

'Hold on, we're just patching in the Director out of Amsterdam.' Lora was seated next to the Professor, and she adjusted the camera so that Alex and Shiva could see better.

'Eva!' Alex said, seeing his friend sitting in on the call too, all the way over on the other side of the Atlantic.

'Hey, Alex!' Eva said. 'How're you doing?'

'Never been better,' he smiled. 'Just dodging danger at every turn and doing my bit to save the world from evil. All in a day, right? How about you?'

'Oh, same as usual,' she said. 'Still waiting for my awesome dream that they reckon I'll have any day now.'

'Yeah, gotta admit, I'm not holding my breath about me having my last 13 dream either. Could be a load of old baloney, if you ask me,' Alex said.

Do I really mean that? I hope that's not true.

'Alex,' the Professor interrupted, 'It's wonderful to see you safe and sound. I hear there are some promising developments from the field.'

'Roger that, Professor, and you too, Director,' Alex said, seeing the screen now divided into three locations—he and Shiva in New York, the Academy in London, and the Enterprise contingent in Amsterdam. 'We've been here in Manhattan, that is, Shiva and me—'

'I,' Eva said.

'Huh?' Alex said.

'It's—'

'We understand,' the Director said. 'Are you two OK?'

'We're fine, *now*,' Alex replied. 'Had a little run-in with our friends Stella and Matrix. It's cool though, we handled it, pretty awesomely too if I may say so. Shiva?'

'I'd say so too,' Shiva chipped in. They could see the Director smiling.

He's taking that as a win for the Enterprise. I guess I really am one of them now.

'It's like we entered "Expert Mode", right?' Alex said, making a private joke with his friend. 'I mean, the way you rode that motorbike, and then we were like argh! and then we took out Matrix, like, whack! and then we had a few seconds, and Matrix was all, "Argh, I'm gonna die", and we got him to stop the bomb and—'

'And do you know what he was up to with the Tesla Coils?' the Director asked.

'Well, yes, we think so, sir,' Alex replied, coughing and straightening up. 'I—we believe he was planning on somehow interfering with the Four Corners Competition.'

'Really?' the Professor leaned in, concern etched on his face. 'So, that's their plan.'

'Looks like,' Alex replied. 'And who knows how far they've gotten with it, *or* how they're going to manipulate it.'

'Or why,' added Eva.

SAM

Taking the nearest flight of stairs, they arrived on the next level down where they came to a control room of sorts. It was a glass box that overlooked inky blackness that their flashlights could not penetrate. Sam figured it was some sort of underground storeroom, and that it was vast.

I guess here's as good a place to start as anywhere. Maybe something will jog his memory.

'What was this place?'

'A government outpost,' Issey said, looking about the room for anything of use. 'I'm not sure if it was military or civilian. It was one of those places that they could go to in the event of a war or catastrophe and live underground for a long time. On my school trip, they said there were provisions here for thousands of people to live out a nuclear winter, maybe even for a hundred years.'

'Great, another one of *those* places . . .'

'You've been somewhere like this before?'

'Yeah, once or twice,' Sam said, then he stopped at a wall and shone his light on a laminated poster. It was a schematic of the facility.

'Here,' Issey said, tapping the elevation plan. 'This is us. The room we're looking out over is the main living quarters. There's an internal greenhouse, recreation areas, sleeping quarters all around it over three levels . . . and here, the storage areas branch off it on the western side, and they go down to sea level.'

'Does this help? Sam asked.

'Yes, I can see from this it's in the storage area,' Issey said, walking away from the diagram and looking out the window at the seemingly infinite abyss of darkness. 'I remember passing rooms filled with supplies in my dream.'

Sam looked at Issey's face in the reflection in the glass.

He looks more certain now.

'We have to keep moving,' Sam said, opening a door to a balcony with a gangway stretching across the three-storey void. 'Stella and her thugs are in here somewhere—they'll be searching too, but only *you* know exactly where the Gear will be.'

I hope that's true . . .

'Then I'll lead,' Issey said, genuine confidence returning to his voice. He started off at a jog and then a flat-out run.

'Maybe we should be a bit quiet—OK, whatever,' Sam muttered as he broke into a run to keep up with the disappearing Issey.

The steel gantry rattled under their footfalls and the echoes reverberated through the concrete cavern.

Sam cringed at the sound but knew they had little

choice—it would take too long to cross the expanse before them if they were stealthy. He imagined how they would look to anyone looking for the source of the commotion—two figures, easily spotted by their flashlights, charging through the darkness. It would seem like they were running through the air.

And if Stella is down here, she can probably hear us too.

And see us.

PING!

A dart ricocheted off the handrail just behind Sam.

Man, I hate it when I'm right!

More hit the underside of the bridge—Stella's thugs *were* below them.

'Keep low!' Sam shouted, and they ran in a crouch. 'And turn off your torch!'

Darkness fell all around them, cloaking them.

They continued on at a jog, Sam with his hand on Issey's back as he ran straight ahead with his hands out in front of him.

Sam could hear whooshes through the air as the darts continued to fly their way, missing the bridge as their attackers fired blindly into the dark, their lights failing to reach them.

'We're close!' Issey said.

PING!

Issey stopped abruptly, Sam crashing into his back.

'There's a door,' Issey said, 'but it's locked.'

PING! PING!

Sam felt around the door itself. Like that at the other end of the gangway, it was made of timber.

'Stand back!' Sam said. He felt the handle again, made a mental picture in the dark of where his target was, then took a couple of paces back. He forced himself to concentrate and ignore the darts that continued to ping and whoosh around him. He approached the door and threw out his leg, his heel connecting with the wood next to the handle.

Not much happened other than Sam reverberating with the impact as his body absorbed as much of the blow as the door. He tried again, and again, and again, each time more frantically.

Come on!

And then—

CRACK!

The door splintered around the lock and another kick later—

SMASH!

The door flew open.

WHACK! WHACK!

Darts pounded into Sam's backpack, one bouncing from his Stealth Suit arm.

'Let's move!' Sam said, flicking on his flashlight as they entered.

The room was empty.

'This isn't right,' Sam said. 'The plans showed a passage

leading down below the level in the main chamber, to the storage cells.'

'There's nothing here but the door we came in through,' Issey said, looking around the small square room. 'And this switch by the door.'

Sam inspected the switch—it seemed unusual, like a big industrial lever of some sort.

Then he looked at the floor. It wasn't concrete, like the walls and the ceiling, it was a steel plate. Around the edges, it didn't quite touch the walls. There was a shadow line, a gap, big enough to put his thumb in.

'Your dad's friend, the superintendent,' Sam said. 'Do you think he turned all the power on when he brought the elevator online for us?'

Issey seemed confused by the question. 'Well, yes. He knew we had to go down here, though I doubt any of these old lamps still work—this place hasn't really been used for over fifty years.'

'Then how about you flip that switch?'

'You sure?'

'Yes,' Sam said.

'But the light—it will show them where we are, they will be coming for us,' Issey protested.

'I don't think that's a light switch,' Sam replied.

Issey, curious, pulled down on the lever.

The floor moved—*down*.

They were standing on top of a massive cargo elevator.

'How do we know which floor to get off on?' Issey said.

'We don't,' Sam said, 'but we'll have—look out!' he ducked, pulling Issey down with him.

WHOOSH!

A net blasted from a launcher shot over their heads as they cleared the floor of the main warehouse level, the side doors facing the shaft having been prised open by Stella's men. They passed a concrete slab that was a metre thick, and then their flashlights revealed a maze of subterranean rooms and corridors. The elevator continued downwards.

'This floor!' Issey said, scrambling on his hands and knees to get off at the next level, Sam rolling out after him.

'Run!' Sam said. 'Follow your gut and run, they'll be close behind us!'

Issey's feet skidded as he ran by a corridor and then did a double take, jogging back to where they'd just been. He stood still for a moment, as though waiting for something.

'What is it?' Sam asked.

'A noise . . . hear that?'

Sam listened. He heard the thrum of many feet running on the level above. 'They're closing in on us,' Sam said. 'Come on, let's go.'

'No, it's not them. It's water, this way,' Issey said, heading down a corridor that curved around in a huge sweeping arc. Sam shrugged and followed him.

I've got to trust him, otherwise we'll never find the Gear.

'Hear it?' Issey said.

'Yeah, so?' Sam said. 'The Gear! We need to find the Gear!'

'It's here.'

'Huh?'

Issey stopped running. Before him was a series of doors, each labelled in Japanese. The stencilled words were spray-painted on.

'What do they say?' Sam said.

'This one is storage—it says it's from after the Second World War,' Issey said. 'And these say they're from a museum,' he added, pointing at others. 'But the Gear is not here, it's further up, follow me.'

Along the corridor, the sound of flowing water grew louder, and at a junction they came to a wall made from criss-crossing metal bars where a torrent of stormwater flowed out to sea on the other side.

'It's here!' Issey said, standing by a closed door next to the drain. 'But it's locked.' Issey took a step back and then—

SMASH!

He kicked the door and bounced off it, his body rocking in pain.

'OK, no, I can't . . .' Issey said, doubling over.

'Ah, Issey?' Sam said, turning the handle and the door clicked open. 'You were turning it the wrong way.'

'Oh, right,' he grimaced.

Inside the room, Sam tried the overhead lights but they blew out in a shower of sparks as soon as he flicked the switch. By the light of their torches, they scanned the room. It was filled floor-to-ceiling with wooden crates, each about the size of a family refrigerator, arranged neatly, with military precision. It looked like there were hundreds of them. The walkways between the crates were tight canyons, like a scale model of a city grid.

'Tell me the Gear isn't packed away in the far corner and under like six of these crates?' Sam said.

'Yeah, that would be a pain . . .' Issey said.

He ambled forwards, and Sam kept checking behind them, a creeping feeling running up his spine that they were being followed.

'Ah, Issey, wanna hustle it along some?' Sam said.

'Trying . . .' Issey said, paused at a crate. It was marked with heavy black Japanese characters.

'What's it say?'

'Military storage,' Issey said. 'Doesn't say what's in there. They're old though.'

'Right. And the Gear?'

'I think it's not in here.'

'But—really?' Sam said, his confidence in Issey starting to waver.

'I . . . I don't know,' Issey said. He looked around the room. Sam could see that he had a pained expression on his face, a look that grew more strained with each passing, panicked second until he clutched at his temples.

Sam caught him as he slumped to the ground, unconscious.

Issey!

EVA

There was silence for a while. Then the Professor spoke. 'If that is true, that she plans to break into the Dreamer Doors construct, then you have alerted us to something very serious.'

'Shiva, Alex, there should be a team of Agents there for your protection any moment,' the Director said. 'Keep the doors barricaded until then.'

'OK,' Alex said.

There was noise from somewhere off screen, and Eva saw Agents entering the complex on the closed-circuit camera feed Jedi was streaming alongside the image of Shiva and Alex.

'Yep,' Alex said. 'They're here now.'

'And Stella?' the Professor asked. 'Do we know her whereabouts?'

'I'm afraid not,' the Director said. 'Not since Tokyo when she chased Sam and Issey. But how about the Coils?'

'It looks like they've made real headway,' Shiva said. 'This should now be considered a real possibility, and a threat in the wrong hands. Looks like I was right all along,' he smiled.

'Yes, indeed, Shiva, noted,' the Director smiled back.

'Are you saying that Tesla's work really could . . ?' the Professor asked.

'Yes,' Alex and Shiva replied at the same time, grinning at each other. 'Jinx!'

'What are we talking about?' Eva asked.

'If I may,' Lora said, 'I believe we're discussing how Tesla worked on harnessing the energy created by our dreamwaves. The energy that, legend has it, the Egyptians were the first to harness through their obelisks.'

'The first and the last,' the Professor said. 'Tesla's machines never worked. He rediscovered the theory, nothing more.'

'What about at the Washington Monument?' Alex said. 'That was to tap into the same thing, wasn't it?'

'Yes,' the Director said. 'But it looks like when you stopped Mac's men, you just stalled the process.'

'Stalled how?'

'Let's go back a step,' the Director said, bringing up images of obelisks. 'These are Cleopatra needles, and here are other obelisks—in New York, Rome and Paris. They were the original transponders.'

'The tallest structures for an age, until they built the pyramids and then their lighthouse in Alexandria,' Shiva added.

More images flashed up.

'Exactly. When the lighthouse was dismantled, the Great Pyramid at Giza was the tallest man-made structure until the Eiffel Tower was built.'

'Which was also a receiver,' Eva added, 'above the Council chambers.'

'Correct,' the Professor said.

'Later,' the Director said, bringing up the images of the Eiffel Tower, 'the Dreamer Council had receiving towers built into newer, taller structures. Those that would have more reach, more capability—'

Pictures of the Washington Monument, the Empire State Building, and skyscrapers from Shanghai to Abu Dhabi flashed across their shared screens.

'In more ways than one,' the Professor interjected.

'Ah yes,' the Director said. 'It's long been suspected in some circles—'

'Widely believed by learned minds,' the Professor added.

'OK, well, *believed*, that the Ancient Egyptians also had the means to *transmit* dreams, not just receive them,' the Director said. 'What's really incredible is that if that were true, you'd think that surely we'd be able to do it by now.'

'But Tesla really was a unique kind of genius,' the Professor said. 'You can have all the technology in the world, but if you can't figure out how to use it . . .' he shrugged.

'Well, we're working on it,' Shiva grinned.

'Do you really think it could become operational now?' the Professor asked.

'With the advent of taller and taller skyscrapers, satellite communication, microwave towers, cell phones, the world is now completely connected to the receiving grid,' Shiva said.

'But that's receiving,' Alex said, 'not *transmitting*.'

'Exactly,' the Director said. 'But that could all be different now.'

'Well,' Eva said, 'like it or not, it looks like we're at that point. Ready or not, the world is about to realise who and what we are and what we can do.'

Five minutes later Eva sat on the edge of Lora's desk in her temporary office. It was clearly usually a library, crammed wall-to-ceiling with bookshelves overflowing with old leather-bound volumes.

Lora pointed to the television where the news was replaying a shot of a yellow sports car slinging off a ramp and then smashing down to a park below and two figures running from the scene.

'I'm so relieved to see Sam and Issey are OK,' Eva said.

Footage of Stella being arrested from the bank of the pond and being put into the back of a patrol car now played. The news cut to a reporter showing the same cop car smashed into a tree and the officers stunned and dazed as they tried to explain how their suspect had overpowered them and escaped into the night.

'I can't believe Stella got away from the cops. And what about Sam?' Eva said.

'Tobias called in to say they were on their way to retrieve Issey's Gear,' Lora said. 'But I'm worried that . . .' her voice trailed off, and she turned up the volume on the television. The news showed live footage from Japan.

'As you can see,' the news anchor said, 'from our helicopter in the sky, which we expect to have to ground at any minute due to the worsening weather, there is some kind of battle raging below on what is known locally as Ghost Island.'

Eva watched wide-eyed as plumes of fire erupted on the island below and tiny figures ran from it. She knew then that Solaris was there. And that Sam was already back in serious danger.

SAM

Sam dragged Issey down an aisle and to an exit door at the nearest corner of the warehouse, where he stopped and sucked at the stale underground air.

He propped Issey up against the wall and could see that he was mumbling and starting to wake up.

There were voices and movement around them.

Stella's Agents.

Then, more worryingly, another noise.

A non-human noise.

It started with a deep, guttural growl. And then another.

There were two of those beasts.

'Monsters are only in dreams,' Sam said to himself. 'They're only in dreams . . .'

A shrill cry echoed out, then the patter-patter of Stella's Agents firing fast and blind, seemingly missing most of anything as they made a hasty retreat. Sam could make out the thudding of the darts hitting the wooden crates.

The beasts gave out a blood-curdling howl.

People screamed out in the darkness.

'Sam . . .' Issey said, his voice hoarse.

'Issey, what happened? Can you move?' Sam whispered, crouching down to his friend and helping him up to his feet.

'I'm sorry . . . panic attack, I can't control . . .' he stammered.

If he was panicked before, we're in real trouble now. I've got to get him out of here.

'The Gear . . .' Issey mumbled.

'Forget it, this is do or die, and we're *not* going to get eaten today,' Sam said.

'No, it's here . . .'

'Issey, come *on*,' Sam urged, leading him through the exit, a thin metal door that Sam shut behind them. 'Let's leave while we can. We can fight another day.'

'I . . . I saw something from my dream, just then when I blacked out,' Issey said.

'What?' Sam leaned Issey against the corridor wall, peering around the corners of a cross-intersection before deciding which way to proceed. He saw five of Stella's guys running—*from* something.

Sam ducked around a corner and led Issey another way. 'What did you dream?'

'It's here,' Issey said. 'It's down one more level.'

Sam stopped them again at the next corner of the maze of walkways.

Perhaps it was built this way in case the fort was overrun, so defenders could hold their positions around blind corners.

Whatever was the case, Sam hated that he just had his little flashlight to lead the way, Issey's arm over his shoulder for support, all the while facing corner after corner where who-knew-what could be lurking.

'Issey, you're not well, we need to be out of here,' Sam said.

'*No*, I saw it,' Issey said, sounding a little more alert with each passing second. 'I saw him get it.'

'Who?'

'That man—that fire-breathing man who fought Kaga.'

'Solaris. You saw him *here*?' Sam asked.

'Yes.'

A shiver ran down Sam's spine. He checked behind them and then ahead, then around the corner. All clear.

'You're sure?'

'Yes.'

'Down one level?'

'Yes. One.'

'And where?'

'It's right there, in a command room, an admiral's office, I think.'

'And the Gear's just sitting there?' Sam couldn't quite believe it.

'Yes, among a heap of other things, part of a collection of old nautical instruments,' Issey said. 'And there's something else.'

'What else?'

'Solaris was not alone. The Gear was given to him, by a woman—short, strong, with a cruel face. The woman from Tokyo, right?'

'Right. Stella,' Sam said. He checked the dark corridors around them again. Sam had to pan the thin beam of the torch side-to-side to see the width of the corridors, and even then he felt he was missing more than he could actually see.

Still all clear.

'Come on, Issey, lead us downstairs to this office,' Sam said.

They turned a corner and Sam stopped, the abrupt halt almost causing Issey to topple them both over.

It was *not* all clear.

In the sweep of the torch beam, Sam had seen something, only his mind hadn't registered it at first because he'd been looking for people chasing them.

But he *had* seen something.

He'd seen eyes.

Two big green-yellow eyes, looking right at them.

Hunting them.

Sam brought the dart gun up in one hand, the flashlight in the other. Both were shaking as the beast charged at him.

Its jaws opened in a massive snarl, wide enough to wrap around his head. It was all frothing saliva and mad, crazed eyes.

Sam steadied. Aimed.

Fired.

The dart went high.

He fired again—the beast leaped to the side, the dart zinging through empty air, then it pounced forward with a new surge of speed, lunging at Sam.

Sam stood still. He focused down the sights of the pistol. At the near end, above his grip, two little white dots were visible in the gloom. Sam struggled to get the little round dot at the front of the barrel to line up in the gap between them. At the last moment, he got all three dots in a row pointed steadily at the beast's large, bobbing head, just a heartbeat away—

Sam squeezed the trigger.

WHACK!

The dart struck the beast in its chest just as it jumped at Sam and its paws hit his shoulders, hard, pounding him down onto the ground and knocking the air out of him.

'Issey, little . . . help . . .' Sam managed to say with the beast lying heavily across him.

Issey rolled the creature off Sam and helped him up.

They looked down at the unconscious animal, shocked at the close call.

'It's just a *dog* . . .' Sam said, incredulous as he looked at the enormous guard dog.

'Not just a dog,' Issey said, crouched down. 'This thing *is* like a monster . . . I've never seen one so big.'

'But it's not some mythical beast,' Sam said, looking around, wary of more dogs coming out of the gloom.

'I, um,' Issey stood back from it, 'think it's not really out cold.'

The huge animal started twitching—first its legs, then its eyes were fluttering, its lips drawing back to reveal huge teeth.

'Maybe dart it again?' Issey suggested.

Then a terrifying and now-familiar howl rang out through the concrete maze.

'Another one?' Issey said. 'Oh boy . . .'

'At least one, maybe more,' Sam said, staring into the dark. 'Let's get out of here!'

At the next turn in the tunnel, Issey stopped at a set of stone stairs leading to a thick, ornate door.

'This is it!' Issey said.

The door was locked.

'Wait a minute,' Sam said, and he unloaded his dart pistol, turned the range setting to maximum and pointed the barrel point blank at the lock.

'What are you doing?' Issey said. 'It's not loaded.'

'I'm hoping the gas charge is enough to blast through the lock. It's gotta be pretty old,' Sam said. 'Hold the flashlight steady and watch out.'

BANG!

The force of the gas hitting the lock blew the pistol from his hand.

'Open sesame!' Sam said, kicking the door.

He bounced off, falling to the ground.

Issey helped him up.

'We're not having much luck with doors, are we?' Sam grimaced, dusting himself off. The door and its lock were undamaged, and his pistol was now empty of gas and useless.

'Argh!' a woman ran through the corridor behind them, her clothing ablaze, oblivious to them. As she passed, her dart gun clattered to the floor.

'One of Stella's guys,' Sam said calmly.

'She . . . she was on fire!' Issey said, too stunned to move.

'She'll be OK, her Suit will protect her,' Sam said, bending down and picking up the gas rifle, which was warm to the touch. 'And more importantly, she left us a parting gift.'

Sam unloaded the weapon and turned the gas to full.

'But—but why was she on fire?' Issey said.

'My guess,' Sam replied, shouldering the weapon and taking aim up against the lock, 'is that just like you dreamed, Solaris has crashed the party.'

Sam pulled the trigger.

The kickback from the rifle firing at full force against the lock sent him crashing into the wall behind him.

'Yes!' Issey said.

The lock was no more—it, the handle and a decent chunk of the door had been blown away.

'This is it!' Issey said, entering the room, and Sam was a pace behind him.

The room was a stately office, wood-panelled and with a smell that reminded Sam of the ancient library underneath the Vatican.

'It's somewhere along here . . .' Issey said, using the flashlight to search the wall.

The room was suddenly illuminated with a bright orange light, gone as quick as it had appeared. Sam heard the familiar *WHOOSH!* that had accompanied it.

'Quick, Issey!' Sam said.

'Here!' Issey took the Gear off a shelf and blew off the dust. 'This is it!'

'We're outta here!' Sam said, and they dashed out of the room to the corridor.

Sam reloaded the dart rifle and turned to see Solaris down the hallway, a darker shadow among the darkness.

Sam didn't hesitate, his gun flying up. He shot Solaris three times in the back.

THUD! THUD! THUD!

CLICK!

The dart gun was empty.

Solaris turned. Sam could not possibly tell, but somehow he could swear that behind that face mask, Solaris was smiling.

'Well, well,' Solaris said in the familiar metallic voice. 'Still with fight in you. One day you'll learn that flight is often the better choice. Then again, your days are numbered, so perhaps that's a lesson that will go unlearned.'

'My days number more than yours, Solaris,' Sam said.

Gotta get the Gear out of here . . .

'Hmm. But think, where would you be without me?' Solaris said. 'Oh yes, that's right, you'd be buried in rubble back in Denver. Not a very pleasant place to die, really. That altitude, the cold. Give me somewhere warm and dry any day.'

'You'll get yours,' Sam said, 'and sooner than you think.'

Solaris chuckled.

'*I'll* take that,' Stella said, emerging from behind Solaris. Dart gun readied, she walked over to Issey and wrenched the Gear from his unwilling grasp. He scowled at her but there was no mistaking his fear.

He's had one hell of a day.

Solaris looked to her, then nodded.

'Take him,' Solaris said to Stella. 'Wait for his next dreams, then send your team to find the last Dreamers and Gears. I'll hold off the others.'

Stella nodded and turned to Sam with an evil look in her eyes. 'I'll keep this one locked away, and we'll meet at the end.' She turned to Solaris. 'Agreed?'

Solaris was silent, then said, 'Do you really think I am a fool?'

Stella's face changed. Now *she* was scared. She backed away a step from Solaris, who seemed to grow in size. Not that he really needed to—he was already almost half a body taller than Stella.

'*I* don't work for *you*,' Solaris said to her. 'And Sam is more important than any Gear. You really think I'd let you take him? You don't even know when you're being tested, do you?'

Stella looked confused and glanced from Solaris to Sam.

'Oh, he can't help you,' Solaris said. 'Then again, I do have a use for you, Stella, what with all the trouble you give the others trying to get these Gears. Look, be a good girl and run along.'

Solaris took the Gear right out of her hands.

Sam could see the fear and rage flickering across Stella's face. She hesitated for a long moment . . .

Are they going to turn on each other?

But she wrestled control of her palpable rage, turned on her heel and stalked away down the corridor, glancing back with fury in her eyes.

Solaris turned the Gear over and over in his hands. 'So, Sam, where were we?' he said. 'Oh yes, your fate . . .'

ALEX

Alex double-checked the video screen showing the Agents outside and called out to Shiva, 'They're here!'

'Let them in!' Shiva called back. 'I'm still re-routing the link back to Matrix's HQ, trying to get their location.'

Alex went to the heavy steel door and lifted the bars to let in the Enterprise Agents—and was promptly knocked flat onto his back.

'Secure the area!' Alex heard shouted over him, a boot pressing down on his chest to keep him pinned.

Alex kicked out hard and fast, the attacker above him doubling over with the blow to his groin. As he scrambled to his feet, Alex managed to duck under a punch and he landed one of his own, and then another, dropping the next two hefty guys to the floor—

WHACK!

Alex was knocked down again. But he forced himself onto his hands and knees, and heaved deep breaths to try to regain focus. He looked up and saw a short guy, along with a couple of tough-looking thugs behind him. They were dressed like Enterprise Agents—but it was just a disguise for the security cameras to gain entry. Their Stealth Suits now changed to black combat gear. Alex craned around to see Shiva and caught sight of him slumped over on his chair. Matrix was similarly hunched over, both of them already knocked out.

Alex turned to face their leader. He looked rich, dressed in a shiny suit with a cravat at the collar.

Is that who I think it is?

'And you are?' he said.

'My name is Hans.' The man paused, as if waiting for recognition.

The guy in Germany who betrayed Dr Dark . . . the treasure hunter!

'Is that supposed to mean something to me?' Alex said, playing dumb. 'To impress me?'

'I guess not,' Hans said, smiling. 'But I would like to impress you, as you have me.'

'Oh?'

'Yes, Alex, what we've seen of you over the last weeks is extraordinary. You are a gifted Dreamer, and I have the means to allow you to reach your full potential.'

'Huh?'

'Here, let's start this introduction again,' Hans said, offering his hand to help Alex to his feet. A little reluctantly, Alex took it and stood, then dusted himself off, glaring at the thug who'd dropped him.

'So what do you want? And why'd you hurt my friend?'

Alex asked Hans, gesturing to the now snoring Shiva.

'I mean him no harm, he is just surplus to my requirements. I am here to see you. I want nothing other than to see you succeed, Alex,' Hans replied. 'I want to see you be the best Dreamer that you can be—that you *ought* to be. Allow me to fund and facilitate your success, to help and guide you in any way that I can.'

'You what?'

And why?

'Alex, I want to see you be a hero.'

So that's his play, is it?

'And just how can you do that?'

'Because, well, let's just say that I'm rich beyond my wildest dreams, *and* yours,' Hans said, smiling. 'And I have *this*.' Hans held out an ancient-looking leather bound journal.

Alex recognised the stamped mark on the front—it was the maker's mark of Leonardo da Vinci. He stared at it and tried to hide his surprise and shock.

This was in the Professor's office at the Academy! How'd he get it?

'Interested?' Hans smiled.

There must be a traitor at the Academy. I need to find out who it is.

'Sure, why not?' Alex smiled back.

SAM

Sam let off the small smoke grenade he'd been cradling in his right hand and rushed at Solaris in one, fluid movement.

I can't see in this—but neither can he.

Sam moved with purpose, hitting Solaris hard in the chest plate, feeling for the Gear in Solaris' outstretched hand.

Solaris caught Sam's wrist in a vice-like grip. 'You think I can't see, *boy?*'

Sam suddenly realised Solaris' tinted goggles might enable him to see in all kinds of conditions. Sam twisted away at the same time as kicking down at where he imagined Solaris' knee to be, connecting hard and breaking free, backing away fast.

But the Gear also fell free. It landed on the concrete floor with a *TINK!*

Let the Gear go. Get out while Solaris finds it. Get Issey out of here.

'Issey!' Sam said, turning and moving away from Solaris. 'Run for the elevator!'

'Good move, boy!' Solaris said, emerging from the smoke—

WHACK!

Sam was knocked to the ground, and he rolled through it and faced Solaris, his shoulder aching.

Solaris' arm was raised—he was about to fire some kind of new weapon at Sam.

Great, now what?

In his other hand he held the Gear, which he thrust into a fold of his armour.

Sam feigned a move to the right and then ducked down to sweep out a kick along the floor, tripping Solaris over.

They were up at the same time, squaring off.

'You really shouldn't have done that,' Solaris snarled.

'I think you started it,' Sam countered.

Solaris didn't reply, but he moved so fast, all Sam saw was a blur and then he was on his back.

As Sam looked up into the black mask from so many of his nightmares, Stella emerged from the smoke.

'Cop this,' she said to Solaris, shooting him with her dart gun point blank in the neck.

Solaris spun around and lashed out fast, knocking Stella away. He pulled the dart from his suit. He looked at it, felt at the puncture wound, then stumbled to his knees.

'Armour piercing,' Stella said, raising her weapon again.

Sam didn't wait around to see what would happen next—he turned and ran.

The maze seemed empty as Sam desperately searched for stairs that led up. He couldn't find any, instead going deeper into the island complex. He paused at a junction and considered for a moment heading back the way he'd come.

No, can't turn back and head towards Solaris and Stella. There must be a way out down here.

OK, left or right?

He went left and soon heard a roaring of water, which he followed to its source. Another junction, but this one was very different—it was a vertical shaft splitting through the tunnel, with stormwater cascading down from above and a steel ring ladder set into a wall. He could get around it, but it seemed the tunnel narrowed and headed down. He reached out to the ladder and stopped.

He looked up.

The drain might lead up to ground level, and I can try to get out that way. Tobias might be up there but maybe bad guys are up there too?

Sam looked down.

Follow the water? It must go out to the sea and Issey's parents should be waiting for us in the boat.

Sam looked up and down, weighing the options.

He went down.

The water's gotta lead out of this rock someplace.

As he followed the water for a few minutes, he dug around in his backpack and checked his phone for a signal. There was still none.

He kept walking, the fast-flowing water up to his ankles. He came to another vertical shaft, this one immense and star-shaped.

I know I've seen this pattern before. Think!

Yes! It was the main stormwater grate, near the base of the watchtower. That's near the elevator . . .

Head up here, get straight to Tobias.

Sam climbed.

As he went higher, his phone found reception again and chimed. He ignored it until he got to the top, where he clambered out and found himself alone at the bottom of the tower. He threw himself towards the base as the echo of gunfire rose above the howling wind and rain. Sam could see several fires burning to either side of him.

What happened here? Where is everyone?

Sam risked pulling out his phone. He had five missed calls from Tobias. Then his phone rang again.

It wasn't Tobias.

EVA

'**S**am?' Eva said into the phone.

'Yeah, I can hear you,' Sam said, his voice strained.

'I can barely hear you. Are you OK?' Eva said.

'Yeah . . . just can't really talk now.'

'I know—I'm watching the news!'

'News?' Sam's confusion was obvious.

'The island in Japan? There are helicopters flying around there, filming. Can't you see them, hear them?'

Eva could imagine Sam looking up at some of the little buzzing lights in the dark sky. The snap-crackle of gunfire continued to provide a background soundtrack over the phone.

'Oh, wow,' Sam said. 'So I'm on TV again.'

'There are Guardians on the island now, trying to help. Can you get to them or get out of there?'

'I haven't seen them yet, but it's hard to see anything. And I got separated from the others. I've gotta find Tobias and Issey first.'

Eva looked at the concrete watchtower on the news

footage. She imagined all that stood in the way of Sam and danger was his dart pistol.

And his bravery.

'I can't leave them . . . there's Stella, and Solaris,' Sam said. 'I gotta go.'

'Head to the east of the island, away from the firefight,' Eva said.

'Got it.'

The gunfire seemed to pause, and all that Eva could hear over the rain was the sound of the helicopters.

'What's happening?' Eva asked.

'No idea. Out of bullets, I hope.'

'Where'd you see Solaris last?'

'Down in the corridors,' Sam said, then paused. 'It's weird—he seems so familiar now. Scary, sure, but I—I'm not as afraid of him anymore.'

'You've dreamed of him so much. You've faced him before.'

'More than that. It's almost as though . . .'

'As though . . .'

'I don't know. Don't you wonder who's behind that mask?'

'Yes.'

'I mean, think about it—that full face mask. Why? Who's behind it? What's he hiding? Is it someone we know?'

'What are you saying?' Eva's heart was pounding.

'It *could* be someone we know.'

'Sam, this is crazy talk.'

Gunfire resumed, a couple of shots, then a whole bunch in reply.

'OK, I'm outta here,' Sam said, scrambling for cover.

'Be careful,' Eva said. 'The Professor is working with the Japanese government to get you more help.'

Sam's phone beeped with a call waiting.

'Eva, I have to go, Tobias is calling,' Sam said, ending the call.

'Sam, wait—'

SAM

'Sam!' Tobias said. 'Where are you?'

'At the base of the watchtower,' Sam replied.

'Can you make it to that star-shaped stormwater drain?'

Sam laughed.

'What is it?' Tobias said, confused.

'I was just down there.'

'Can you come down again? There's another way out,' Tobias said. 'I just found it, but doubled back to try to find you. Take the water shaft down to the bottom, and then the tunnel that carries the water out to sea.'

'OK.'

'I'll meet you down there. Be quick.'

Sam ended the call and ran around the watchtower towards the water grate. Luckily the way ahead was clear and he knew where to go. The ladder in the shaft was slippery, and he took it fast as he could until he got to the lowest level. He ran down the western tunnel, following the water's flow out to the sea, and stopped and waited.

There was a dim light behind him. Then, he heard a noise.

Running, splashing in the water.

A person.

'Sam!'

'Tobias?' Sam turned but the echoes in the tunnel and the darkness made things difficult. 'Is that you?'

'Sam!'

'Over here!' Sam called out.

In a moment Sam could see the illumination of a flashlight and then his friend appeared, soaking wet, like he'd swum ashore to the island.

'We have to keep moving,' Tobias said, hands on his knees, sucking for breath. 'Fast.'

'Issey?'

'He made it down to the pier. They're on the boat headed around to this side of the island.'

'How do we get out?'

'Same way this water does.'

I knew it.

Sam looked at the water rushing through the tunnel at his feet.

Tobias rested in a heap next to Sam, his back against the wall, still breathing heavily. He looked to Tobias again.

He looks like he's been wrestling underwater sea monsters.

'Solaris?' Sam asked.

'I saw him back up top,' Tobias said. 'He seemed stunned, but still able to shoot pretty well.'

Tobias showed Sam a huge black and blue welt on his neck that must have been from Solaris' new weapon.

'Stella darted him,' Sam said, and explained what happened.

'Well,' Tobias said. 'Solaris is still groggy, but not for long. He was throwing his fire around everywhere. I got out just as the local authorities used a helicopter with one of those huge fire-fighting buckets to douse us. He got the worst of it, though it swept us both down into that stormwater drain back there.'

Sam said, 'I wish it had washed him out to sea.'

'Maybe, but for now, be thankful we're all in one piece,' Tobias said, then stood and readied himself. 'We have to keep moving.'

They were nearly at the end of the water when Sam's phone rang.

'Eva?' Sam said, still using the phone as a flashlight out front and looking at the screen—it wasn't Eva, but it was a number he knew. A number he hadn't seen for weeks.

A number that stopped Sam cold.

Tobias stopped and turned around. 'Sam, what is it?'

'This number . . .' Sam looked at the screen. 'It's my mum's. Jane, I mean. She's calling me.'

Tobias looked at the screen. 'How would she have your Academy number?'

'I don't know. But I should answer it, right?' Sam's voice wavered.

'I'm not sure about that. This could be one of Stella's tricks,' Tobias cautioned.

'She might need my help,' Sam countered.

'It seems so out of the blue. I know Mac knew where they were when you saw them on the screen in Denver. But no-one has heard from them since then.'

'But—I have to answer it.'

Tobias looked behind him to the tunnel exit and faced Sam again. He nodded.

Sam answered the call. 'Mum?'

'No, I don't think so, Sam.'

Stella! Tobias was right!

'But you better come out from down there,' Stella said, 'if you want to see your precious family again.'

'But—how do you have this phone? Where is my family?' Sam said, his voice wavering.

There was the sound of scuffling and a new voice came on the line.

'Sam? Sam, is that you?'

'Mu—Jane . . .' Sam closed his eyes. He wanted to ask, *are you with me? Do you care?* But he couldn't bring himself to do that, not yet.

'Sam, I'm so sorry. Please forgive me,' Jane's voice broke on the line. 'But whatever she says, don't do it! She's just—'

She was abruptly cut off as Stella came back on the line. 'See?' she said. 'Your father and annoying little brother are here too. You can have the three of them in exchange for you. That's not a bad trade is it? One life for three?'

'I don't believe you,' Sam spat out, the blood hammering in his ears.

What do I do?

'You have one minute to consider saving your family. Otherwise we'll be forced to do something that you cannot take back, not even in your dreams.'

The line went dead.

'It's a trap, Sam,' Tobias said.

'But . . .'

'They could be working *with* her. Or, and this is more likely, it might not really be your mum at all.'

Sam's confusion was obvious on his face.

'Think about it, Sam,' Tobias said. 'Stella's got Matrix working with her and had access to Enterprise files. It's possible Matrix has created a sound file for your mother but it's not really her.'

Sam looked into his teacher's eyes, searching for answers that he knew weren't there. 'But what if you're wrong? And what if I'm wrong? Maybe they did love me. And I miss them. All of them.'

'Sam, I know, it's hard . . .' Tobias said, his voice soothing and matter-of-fact. He gestured behind them, where the sound of the sea roared against the rocky cliffs. 'We have a way off this island, but we have to take it now.'

Sam could see the concern on Tobias' face that he'd

seen on his own parents' faces on so many occasions.

'Sam, we can glide out from here, down to the water's edge at the south, using our Stealth Suits—just like you did at the Eiffel Tower, remember?'

Sam nodded.

'Issey is down there, with his parents, in their boat. No-one will see us leaving if we go now while there's still mayhem going on up there. We'll be out of here and we'll be safe. We've already lost the Gear. We can't lose you too.'

'But I can't just *leave* them here with Stella,' Sam despaired.

'You have to understand just how valuable you are, Sam. You cannot allow yourself to fall into the wrong hands. You've almost run out of your nine lives.'

'Thirteen, you mean,' Sam joked feebly. He nodded and wiped away a sniffle. 'This is an impossible choice.'

'And I'm sorry for that, Sam, I really am. Look, if it's true what Stella says, that your parents are not working with her, then Stella won't risk doing anything to them—they're an asset for her to use against you, if not now, then at another time. And that will give us the chance to rescue them later on, OK?'

'So we just leave them here?' Sam asked.

'It's either just them captive, or them *and* you,' Tobias said.

Sam sighed.

'Sam,' Tobias said. '*We're* your family now.'

Sam's phone rang. He watched the incoming call flashing on his screen.

Tobias started walking towards the tunnel that opened out above the sea.

Sam put the phone in his pocket and followed him.

37

The tunnel ended abruptly. It was dark below with only the white-capped waves of an angry sea breaking up the blackness.

'Sam, we're going to have to jump,' Tobias said, looking down the sheer cliff face below.

Sam swallowed hard and looked down past his toes. He'd never liked the taller diving boards at his local pool, and he'd never even tried the ten-metre platform. This was much higher, much scarier and worse than the Eiffel Tower because of the dark, and the water. And bobbing in the dark choppy water was a tiny boat, with the three figures visible, battling against the storm and sea spray. In the deluge of rain it was impossible to make out who they were, but Sam knew that it must be Issey and his parents.

'You need to jump out, as far as you can,' Tobias said, 'glide out, so that you clear the island and any rocky outcrops.'

Sam nodded.

'Aim to hit the water straight, feet first and arms tight

to your sides,' Tobias said. 'You don't want to land flat on your back.'

'OK, OK.' Sam felt like throwing up.

'I'll go first. Once you see me clear and swimming towards the boat, you follow.'

Sam nodded, fixated on the waves below. From the wind and rain of the night, he could not hear the pitter-patter of the gunfire from the battle above, nor the helicopters flying even higher overhead as they searched the island.

My parents . . . what will happen to them?

'Sam!' Tobias took Sam by the shoulders and shook him.

Sam looked into Tobias' eyes. They were full of steely determination.

'Sam—you must do as I said!' Tobias said.

'OK,' Sam said, trembling. 'I'll follow.'

'How will you land?'

'Feet first.'

Tobias nodded and let Sam go. He looked down to the sea, took a few deep breaths and took a running jump, disappearing out into the night.

Sam watched as his friend soared through the sky, heading down, his arms and legs still moving in a running motion at first, and then he opened up his Stealth Suit to glide, his arms out like wings, until he shifted again into a position so that he was falling straight down like a pin.

His feet hit first, his straight legs piercing the sea, then he disappeared under.

Sam scanned the surface of the sea with wide eyes, and then a flashlight from the little boat began searching the water where he'd landed.

Nothing.

Nothing but the raging sea and the tiny boat.

Tobias! Where are you?

Sam scanned the water and saw no sign of him.

Is it too dark to see him?

Tobias emerged, bobbing up in the water like a cork. He looked up to Sam and gave him a wave and thumbs up, then he rolled around and found the boat and settled into a freestyle stroke towards it.

'Yeah!' Sam called out.

Sam stood on the edge of the drain. Water was gushing out over his feet, ankle deep and growing deeper by the second, emptying the top levels of the island from the rain deluge. He hung on tight to the round wall of the pipe, watching as Tobias was hauled out of the water, and a few seconds later saw all four figures in the boat waving at him.

It was his turn to jump.

He took a few steps back, until he felt the steel bars against his back.

'Come on . . .' Sam said to himself. 'You can do this.'

He took some deep breaths, in and out, in and out. He

felt a calm washing over him as he slowed his heart rate and thought through what was ahead—run and jump, clear the island, form a straight pose to enter the water.

Don't fight the entry, float to the surface, swim for the boat.
Piece of cake.

Sam bent over and vomited.

The water was now halfway up his calves and the current strong enough that it was starting to push him out.

He hung onto a bar behind him, bent down, rinsed his mouth and face, then stood up and looked at the black hole full of night sky ahead of him.

'OK, Sam, piece of cake time.'

He took a deep breath, and exhaled.

'One . . . two . . .'

A final settling breath.

'Three!'

Sam let go of the bar and ran.

And went nowhere.

He was caught. The back of his Stealth Suit was snagged somehow.

He looked back into the tunnel behind, but he couldn't see anything, hear anything.

But he felt a presence. He was being watched, stalked.

He saw the shine of the eyes before he heard the growl.

It was one of the huge guard dogs and it was watching him.

Slowly moving towards Sam, confident in knowing that

its next feed was cornered—ready for the slow and brutal mauling.

Sam tugged against his Stealth Suit, but it would not budge. The material was so strong, and the snag so complete, it would never tear free.

The dog stalked towards him. Sam could see its front haunches now, the hair on the back of its neck all prickled up, its ears flattened back. Its mouth opened in a snarl of huge yellow fangs.

Sam slowly unzipped his Stealth Suit, then slipped out a shoulder and then an arm, one after the other, the whole time not breaking the dog's gaze.

He pulled the Suit down past his shorts, removing one leg at a time.

Not for a moment feeling the cold, Sam pulled his last foot out as the dog sprang forwards—

Sam turned and ran.

And jumped.

Sam straightened his body and spread out his arms.

But I don't have a Suit to glide in!

'Arghhh!' Sam drew his bare legs together, his feet pointed down—but it was too late, he had plummeted too fast. Sam landed awkwardly, slapping his back against the sea and feeling all the air blast out of his lungs. A wave washed over him and the inky black of the sea swallowed him whole.

A million needles of pain entered his skin as the cold

water bit hard. The motion in his ears told him he was still descending.

He forced his screaming limbs to work, fighting to come back up. He broke the surface and swam, hard as he could for ten strokes, then stopped to get his bearings.

A bright red-orange light pierced the sky. A flare gun, shooting over his head and hitting the water just behind him.

Sam swam for the boat. It seemed to take forever, even though the boat was also heading for him. His arms and legs were moving in a swimming motion but it was as if he had no control over them. He swam until he felt hands reaching down and curling under his arms, picking him out of the water.

He lay on his back on the deck of the boat, the relieved faces of Issey and his father bent over him. Tobias said something to him, but Sam's ears were not working.

Probably the cold water. Maybe my whole head has turned to an iceblock.

Sam didn't feel warmer when a blanket was placed over him. But with each passing moment, he felt and noticed a little more as his senses slowly returned. Issey remained by his side, and his smiling face was a welcome sight. Sam felt the vibrations of the engine run through him.

We're leaving. We're safe.

Whatever we've been through, we've made it.

The pang of losing the Gear was not far behind his temporary relief.

Who has it now? Stella? Solaris?

Rain continued to fall.

Sam heard a shout, but could not make out the words.

From nowhere, the world around him changed from one of darkness to blinding light.

Fire engulfed the bow of their boat, then another bright jet shot over their heads. A thin, accurate flame.

Solaris!

Issey grabbed hold of Sam, his body shielding him. But the next stream of fire hit the rear engine of the boat, the petrol tank instantly exploding in a violent and devastating blast.

The last thing Sam remembered was floating in the water, face up, the boat gone, fire-soaked debris all around him.

Then everything went dark.